DEAD GROUND

★

By the same author

DEAD GROUND

★ ★ ★

HOWARD CLEWES

E. P. Dutton & Company, Incorporated

New York   1946

TO JOCELYN

★

In military technology, 'dead ground' is country which by virtue of its configuration cannot be subjected to direct aimed fire by the enemy

★

DEAD GROUND

DEAD GROUND

THE ADJUTANT said abruptly, 'For heaven's sake, man, stop crying,' and Spanish the Harbour Commissioner seemed hurt and embarrassed, he having done little more than sniff occasionally and wipe a tear from the corner of his eye. 'It's the co'd wind in me eyes,' he muttered and trotted a little to catch up, for the Adjutant walked very fast, and somewhat erratically, the fine spray in the air continually misting his glasses and blinding him so that he went perilously near the edge once or twice and Spanish said to himself, One of these times he will go over all right. Irritably the soldier wiped the spray from the lenses, but in a moment they would be as bad. They went on down the jetty, the sea very ugly on either side, and when they reached the ship, they stopped. 'There she is,' Spanish said. The Adjutant shouted, 'What d'you say?' above the wind, and Spanish said, 'I said, that's her.' 'Yes,' said the Adjutant testily, so he supposed and thought to himself, the damned old fool. The ship rose now to the swell and he caught a glimpse of the portly hull, festooned with yellow weed and barnacles; then slowly she plunged again, burying some little of her shame in the dark curtain of the water. Rust wandered over her sides like land on a map and the ropes holding her fore and aft had taken root in the boards of the jetty and a trace of grass grew bright green at the base of the capstan. A gull circled over her once, twice, and, with a certain dainty precision, lit on the masthead. For a moment the bird watched keenly the two men on the quay, absently dropped lime on to the already white-splashed deck below, bunched, settled its wings, and squatted and slept. From the thin black funnel aft smoke drifted across the harbour and if you listened you would hear, deep in the belly of the ship, a voice singing.

The deck, when they went up the gangway and aboard, was littered with lengths of black and frayed rope and rusty cable and chains and lobster-pots and planks and mud and gravel where the soldiers had trundled their barrows across to the hatch, left open and yawning to the sky. And everywhere, over everything, there was birdlime white and like a shroud. 'She's in a fair mess,' said Spanish, and added in a moment, 'The military's been at her again.' The Adjutant looked sharply at the Harbour Commissioner and his hand strayed again to the voluptuous moustache, now lank with sea-water, which had the air of having been stuck to his face for purposes of disguise, but Spanish only blinked at the dunes to the north beyond the empty harbour and bent his back to the wind and sniffed. 'What's that singing?' the Adjutant demanded suddenly. 'Singing, sir?' 'Yes, the singing below,' the Adjutant said, he had heard it quite distinctly. Was that the Captain? Spanish said, 'Old Thwaite? Lord, no, sir. That's the Engineer, Edwards. That's Edwards,' he shouted. 'What's he singing for?' Spanish did not know; the Engineer was always singing. 'They reckon he must be fond of music,' he said.

The Adjutant began to curse savagely. He cursed the maddening gusty wind. He cursed the Harbour Commissioner. He cursed the drunken sea-captain, who was the cause of it all; the ship, for its impassive, derelict majesty; the spray, where it stung his over-shaven chin and misted his glasses. He cursed the Commanding Officer, who had said, 'Better run down to the harbour, Billy, and see about the blockship. Get a breath of fresh air. Go on, you haven't been outside the office for ten days,' as though it were his, the Adjutant's own, fault that he had not been out for ten days. And then hurriedly he remembered himself and that he must not think ill of the Commanding Officer, let alone speak it aloud, so he cursed Gerard the Company Commander because that was all right; you could say what you wished of the Company Commander.

'I haven't seen Edwards in months,' Spanish said.

'Why not?'

'He never comes up. Nobody's seen him.' The voice below would begin a song and then maybe stumble on a high note and go back to the beginning and try another key and then go on if it was all right. It seldom got far. 'He lives in the engine-room.'

'What's the matter with him?'

'Matter?' Spanish was surprised. 'Nothing. He's on strike.'

The Adjutant drew a deep breath.

'Won't come up, no matter what. Not till she sails.'

'Bolshie, I wouldn't be surprised.'

'Couldn't tell you about his politics; I never take much interest meself.' The Adjutant said briefly that he was not concerned with the Engineer's political opinions; he was

speaking of a state of mind. 'A state of mind, you understand,' he said. Between the trouser pockets and the sleeves
of the Harbour Commissioner's jersey there was a ring of
purple flesh where the wrists were exposed; it was curiously
repulsive. Indeed, the old man looked altogether so forlorn
and abject and humble that the soldier hated him for it, with
an active physical intensity, as he hated the poor for their
poverty. 'There's only one way to deal with people like
that,' he said.

'Aye, best leave 'em alone.'

'Put 'em up against a wall.'

For God's sake why was it that every time he encountered a civilian the same damned thing occurred? Shut your
mouth, he said to himself, shut up, you clacking fool.
Always he would find himself trying to impress them, to
dominate and silence them with a ferocity palpably spuri-
ous, and succeeding so admirably that it seemed almost as
though he was being led into it, that their humility was
studied, a foil set to inflame the temper of his professional
pride and render it ridiculous.

'Turn a machine-gun on 'em,' he said, grinding his teeth.

'He's published a protest, has Edwards.'

'I daresay. They practically always do.'

The ship rose and plunged slowly and the ropes slapped
at the mast in the wind.

'It's in The Navigator yonder, in the saloon. Very nice
it is. A protest against the Government and the Admiralty
and the owners and injustice generally.' A shower of spume
struck the Adjutant across the face. 'Fourteen months,'

Spanish went on, 'she's been tied to this jetty. Fifteen come my Maisie's birthday. And never moved an inch.'

'Can she?' he asked, but the sarcasm was wasted.

'Supposed to, she is. When the Boche comes. Then she casts off and sails half steam ahead about thirty-five maybe forty yards, then hardaport and full steam astern a bit and there she is slap across the harbour mouth. Make her fast fore and aft to the jetty heads and there's nothing can pass. Ram her and she sinks. But she can't go down far. And for that' — the Harbour Commissioner stared up at the funnel whence a trickle of smoke fled down to the tossing water and over it towards the distant dunes — 'for that she's had steam in her poor old boilers night and day for nigh on fifteen months.' He ran a finger along the tip of his nose. 'Edwards won't come up, not till she sails.'

'Is that where the ballast goes?' He pointed to the open hatch.

'Aye.'

They went to the edge and looked in at the sand and gravel and bricks and salmon-tins and cigarette-cartons.

'Where's the Captain?'

'In the Navigator yonder; he mostly is.'

'I want to see him.'

They left the ship. A single plane droned across the sky towards the sea. It went out a long way and then turned in a full wide circle, shining for a moment like an early star as it caught the last upslanting rays of the sun and headed inland towards the gaunt reservoir on the hill and the squat cottages that stood out flat and black against the western sky. Below them the town sprawled down the dark hillside. One or two points of light winked pleasantly in the High Street where Mark Ramsden and Miss Honeyman and the delicatessen shop, white-tiled like a public lavatory, had not yet closed their shutters. Now and then a dog barked unexcitedly and a long way away a bicycle bell shed a few saccharine tears that drifted out across the harbour towards the lonely ship against the southern jetty.

And on the jetty the sentry, who would soon be relieved, prayed that the officer would not see him or speak to him. Please, Lord, let the bastard go home. I always make such a muck of it. Let him not notice me standing here quietly or inspect my equipment, which is far from clean, or ask me my duties which I do not know, or how I like the army or any damned thing at all. Simply let him go and leave me alone, that is all I want. That surely cannot be much to ask. Oh, please, please.

The Adjutant said, 'What is your name?'

The sentry came clumsily to attention, swaying a little in the wind. 'Elwes,' he answered.

'Sir,' the officer added.

Elwes did not answer. A flush spread over his solemn pink face. He had wide, slow-moving eyes and spoke only with an effort, seeming to pick his way through a jungle of words, stumbling and falling, hurting himself as he moved, and he appeared very shy, so that when you spoke to him he would shrink away from you and his head would move round away from you and the eyes avoid your glance.

'What are your duties, Elwes?'

16

'I have to watch the sea.'

'Yes. What else?'

He hesitated. 'The harbour, sir.'

'Yes. Anything else? What about the sky?'

'Yes, sir. Aeroplanes.'

'And the ship.'

'Yes, sir.'

'You don't seem too sure.' He waited. 'Do you?'

'No, sir.' The wind whipped the long coat against his legs. He stared at the sea, leaning his bayonet towards the near horizon. They lived in the hut with the rusty wire entanglements round it, trampled flat where the track led through it to the little privy; a corporal and six men guarding God alone knew what: the harbour maybe, and the ship and the empty coal-trucks and one thing or another, and for this they had a Lewis gun with its ugly snout now gaping dumbly at the sky. Every day a truck brought them food and sometimes an officer, one of Captain Gerard's subalterns, who said good morning assiduously to everybody he saw, came with it and stayed a few hours. The days were very tedious for the guard, but people gave them cups of sweet tea and cigarettes and books and occasionally they would sight a stray mine going south with the drift and fire off a few magazines at it. They had never hit one, though in truth you had to strike a horn to detonate the charge, but the old gun made a splendid noise, a fine fat crazy din whose echo bounced from the hills like laughter and frightened everybody in the town till they realized what it was and breathed deeply and said, 'It's the guard. Thank God we are guarded, anyway.' Today there had been quite a lot to watch, for some of the men from the reserve platoon had been tippling rubbish into the ship again and Captain Thwaite had come staggering down the jetty to kick them off it. They had heard the hysterical cursing and had seen the old man shove a barrow into the sea.

'What did you do in private life, Elwes?'

Elwes swallowed and his eyes drifted away again. 'I was on the railway, sir.'

'Always?'

'No, sir.'

'What else?'

'I've 'ad a few jobs.'

'I see. Well, you're in the army now.'

'Yes, sir.'

'How d'you like it?'

Elwes swallowed. 'I don't like it, sir.'

'No, I don't suppose you do.' He was somewhat surprised at the man's courage; perhaps it was ignorance only. 'You will, though.'

'Yes, sir.'

'You've a lot to learn yet.'

'Yes, sir.'

'Then hurry up and learn it.'

He turned and went down to the jetty after Spanish, who was waiting for him by the hut where the guard lived. The Corporal, leaning against the door smoking, came reluctantly to attention. The Adjutant was glad he had spoken to the sentry and for a moment considered having a word with the guard commander also and maybe inspecting the billet. It was advisable, he thought, to look into these stray detachments from time to time; you could never trust the company commanders to do so; indeed, you never knew what arrant foolishness these damned civilian soldiers were condoning. Spanish fell in beside him and they went on towards The Navigator. The wind was rising.

In the harbour below the surface the mines tugged at their cables, leaning this way when the tide was flowing, that way with the ebb. There were minefields in the grey dunes; those were land-mines. When you had lived long enough in Imbleness you forgot the mines or grew accustomed to the vague suspense, but at first they lay heavy on the mind, for there were enough in the harbour by sympathetic detonation to blow the town off the hillside and leave the hillside clean. And nearly every day at first there was an explosion in the dunes when a dog strayed through the wire and stepped on a mine. Watson West lost his daughter Eunice there; they found her foot on the beach. So you would catch yourself sometimes flinching when you went near the quay and screwing up the corners of your eyes.

The fishermen did not use the harbour now, though it was considered safe enough for small craft. Instead their women ran out the heavy wheeled carriers called cradles to the white surf to meet the boats and tow them clear and dry up the beach, where they lay with prows rearing to the sky and flat sterns in the sand and the great cradle wheels on either flank; like this, they had the air of ancient chariots.

19

About the cobles now the Adjutant walking down the jetty with Spanish could see the fishermen, Watson West and Roderick his brother and his boy Harry and Jack Elder and the half-witted Jim and Moon and Sellers and one or two more preparing the lines for tomorrow. The women were among them with shawls over their heads or hair streaming in the wind, spreading seaweed on the baited hooks to keep them fresh and stacking the trays and watering the coiled lines so that they would not stiffen and stink and drive away the fish, and some were filling the petrol tanks and bailing out yesterday's bilge water with a lot of splashing. In the night the cobles would go out with the tide and return on the afternoon of the following day for the auction of the catch. Tomorrow, maybe, not all the boats would return, there would be one missing and the women would wait there till night fell again in a small crowd on the dry grey sand watching the flotsam. Presently the lifeboat would go out when enough fishermen to form a crew had returned and presently come back.

Last month Henry West and his son Hugh had struck a mine, nobody knew whether British or German, but it must have been a contact mine, for the coble was built of wood and so could not detonate magnetic mines, and the engine, an old Buick, could hardly have exploded an acoustic mine. They heard the distant boom, all the town heard it, and the windows rattled and people speaking in the streets were silent and nobody moved for a moment, listening. The scraps came in with the next flow, but the lines they had cast were out there now; if you went out a mile or two on a clear day you could see the floats, with glasses. Henry West and his boy had ventured too far into the minefield four or five miles out that ran like a broad belt parallel with the coastline. There was a way through it all right, but nobody knew where it was, anyway not the fishermen. Only the sentry had seen the distant spout, or said he had.

They went on towards the inn. There was scarcely a breath of light left in the sky.

STANDING in the door of the inn Allan Gerard, the Company Commander, watched the two men coming towards him down the jetty, the one briskly and with intent, the other shambling, half-trotting, hands in pockets. Now they were behind and beyond the derelict waggons that stood along the quayside, where, earlier in the evening in the thin yellow sunlight, he had come upon the litter of brats playing shrilly about the boy who had been piddling into the harbour.

In the parlour they looked up when he opened the door and seeing the tall figure outlined against the light fell silent. Those who were playing dominoes, the verger and the mechanic from the reservoir and the man from the garage, bent to their game with a sudden immoderate zeal, but the old sailor in cap and seaboots who sat away from the light stared for a long time at the officer and his lips moved as though he would speak.

He shouted suddenly, 'Uncle O'Hara!' The peak of his cap shone dully and his lips made a faint popping sound as he drew at an empty pipe. Allan Gerard nodded towards him and grinned, but the old man ignored him; he picked up the brass shovel from the hearth and belaboured the fender with it.

'O'Hara!'

There was no answer.

'Service for a sea-faring man!' He stared defiantly at the Company Commander and let the shovel fall into the hearth.

There was a hatch in the wall behind the sailor's chair that gave on to the saloon bar. Now it was flung open and Uncle O'Hara's round damp face was thrust into the room.

'Rum,' the old man said.

'Shut your trap, Captain Thwaite.'

'Get me a rum, I said.'

'Not a drop. And shut up; you're disturbin' the guests.'

'To hell with the guests. Which guests?'

'All of them, Captain Thwaite. The guests takin' their ease be the warm fire in the beautiful hotel lounge amusin' themselves be playin' dominoes and drinkin' a quiet Scotch and contemplatin' the damfool antics of a drunken beach-comber that hasn't seen the sea in God knows how long, let alone sailed the bastard. Shut up.'

'Get me a rum and charge it.'

'You're drunk.'

He withdrew from the hatch and left it like a frame without a picture, for you could see nothing beyond but blue smoke and the light shining in the spilled liquor on the board and O'Hara's belly in profile.

'O'Hara!'

His voice was drowned in the spatter of a running tap and the brisk hiccup of the till.

He muttered wearily, 'It's no use; he can't hear me.'

'He can,' said the verger, who was playing dominoes. 'He can hear you all right.' He knew Uncle O'Hara, knew him well. O'Hara was the choirmaster of St. Thomas's; he had a fine mellow voice and led the children in the choir and indeed all the congregation. He sang with great feeling.

'And what's more, Captain Thwaite,' said O'Hara, thrusting his face through the hatch again, 'if you don't shut up I'll be droppin' a line to the owners, and God help you then, me boy.'

'To hell with the owners.'

'Then I'll be sendin' for your wife then and have you put to bed if you don't shut your trap. Do I make myself clear?'

The old man's head shook and a whine came into his voice. 'Don't tell her, O'Hara. You mus'n' do that. Not that woman.'

And here, for the scene was well rehearsed, O'Hara would rest his dimpled elbows on the frame of the hatch and smile at the old man's back and say, 'Then shut up,' gently. He smiled at Allan Gerard and nodded, and Gerard watched him, faintly sickened by the shining pinkness of the man's face and head and by the deliberate exaggeration of the brogue and the overwhelming friendliness. But Captain Thwaite was either too drunk or too fearful of O'Hara's threat to argue, for he said nothing, only shifted the cap on his head and rubbed the stubble on his chin and peeped at Gerard from under his overhanging brows. In a minute he lit a match and held it erratically to the empty pipe. Upstairs, in the room above, there was somebody moving about. The players shuffled the dominoes on the table.

'No tobacco,' the old man muttered.

'And no rum,' said O'Hara.

With sudden violence Captain Thwaite cried, 'Don't I pay for it?'

'Oh, sure. Sure you do. Or she does maybe. And it's her orders. No rum for Captain Thwaite, she said, not another drop.'

'The bitch,' he whispered, 'the bitch, the dirty bitch.'

''Tis for your own good.'

'I'm in trouble, O'Hara. A man in trouble needs a drink.'

O'Hara nodded. 'The military, no doubt. It's a cryin' shame. The military and the naval authorities and the lovely owners.'

'The military, O'Hara.'

'Ah! 'Tis an invasion they are.'

'I showed the buggers.'

'Did you now? What action did you take?'

'I kicked their arses.' His voice rose shrilly. 'Kicked the buggers off the ship.' He peered at Allan Gerard under his brows. 'Tipping muck into the hold they were, hundreds of them. Muck!' But the officer did not move.

O'Hara smiled pleasantly. 'What kind of muck would it be now?'

'For God's sake what's it matter what kind of muck? Muck, I tell you — that's enough, isn't it? Ballast they call it.' But he knew Allan Gerard would not be drawn. He had known this officer a long time, for he commanded the men who guarded the harbour, and liked him; they understood one another without a word exchanged.

'I understand,' the publican said. 'We all understand, don't we?' There was a murmur of assent from the domino players. Soon now, under the baiting, the old man would begin to weep or maybe the rage in his heart would explode in a crazy jet of words that filled the room and drenched the verger and the engineer and the man from the reservoir with its passion. They appeared unmoved. They listened attentively enough till the torrent slowed to a trickle, a rumbling in the old man's throat, and then stopped, and there was nothing left of him but his loose bulk and blood-shot eyes and trembling fluttering fingers.

A man came into the room quietly and said good evening. The domino players took no notice and Uncle O'Hara withdrew from the hatch. The man came towards the fire rubbing his hands.

'How's business — all right?' he said. He was very small and wore a loose grey moustache and thick glasses and there was dust in the wrinkles of his coat.

Nobody answered his question. He looked at the old man with the fixed intensity of the near blind and wished him good evening. 'Perry is the name,' he said, 'Alexander

Perry.' He lit a cigarette and kept it between his lips so that it protruded exactly from the centre of his moustache and wagged decorously when he spoke.

'Fancy goods, my line,' he said. 'Knick-knacks, you know. Lucky charms.' With a thumb and forefinger he felt in his waistcoat pocket and found one or two small black objects and, placing one of them in the palm of his hand, extended the hand to Captain Thwaite.

'Have one,' he said.

The sailor peered at the small thing in the palm of Perry's hand. 'What's that?'

'A sacred baboon, this one, sir.'

'I've seen them, real ones. Tomato-arsed bastards.'

'I have others. This one, for instance' — he placed another in the palm of his hand — 'is a sacred elephant. Notice the curious configuration of the tusks.'

Captain Thwaite told him to see the Chief Engineer.

'Who, sir?'

The verger said, 'You gave the Captain one last night.'

'Did I indeed? Yes, that is right — yes, I did.' He put the things back in his pocket. 'Yes, I remember now.' He turned away to go to the desk on which he had left his papers and saw Allan Gerard standing in the windows. He touched the soldier's arm.

'Have a lucky charm, sir, just the thing for a soldier.'

'I lack faith, Mr. Perry.'

'Ah, yes. You've got to have faith. Certainly one needs faith. My old governor, I remember, when I first started, said to me, Perry, he said, it's useless to try and sell your goods unless you have faith in them yourself. I have never forgotten that. I was seventeen at the time.' He held out the charm again. 'It's quite free.'

'Thank you, no.'

'I sell a great many of them, you'd be surprised. They're very good, one of my best lines. Very lucky indeed.'

'No.'

The traveller turned away then and shuffled to the desk and moved the papers about and began to write out his orders for the day. The ash fell from the cigarette on to the paper. On the table the dominoes rattled stealthily and in the saloon O'Hara's voice split the wooly murmur as he served the general public and outside the sea whispered monotonously. Allan Gerard waited for the Adjutant.

When the Adjutant and the Harbour Commissioner came in, Captain Thwaite raised his head and, seeing the officer with the dewy moustache and glasses and buttons all glittering sharply in the light, his eyes steadied themselves.

For a moment nobody spoke.

'You get out,' whispered the old man at last.

The Adjutant stood quite still. Spanish sniffed in the silence and his eyes watered.

'Go on, get out.'

The Adjutant ignored him. He asked Allan Gerard, 'What are you doing here?'

'Waiting for you, Billy.'

'Oh! You couldn't act on your own initiative, I suppose?'

The old man said, 'I told you to get out of here.'

'Who are you?' Now the Adjutant turned towards him.

'Were those your men on my ship today?'

'They were on the blockship.'

'My ship.'

'Possibly. Are you Captain Thwaite?'

'Get out.'

The domino players watched them and Allan Gerard listened and in a moment Spanish blurted,

'I've brought in the Adjutant, Daniel.'

'You keep out of this, Spanish.'

'About your ship, Captain Thwaite.' The Adjutant raised his voice, not in anger, though his temper was fraying now, but because the old man was deep in liquor, as he would have raised his voice to a Frenchman because his grammar was impure. He was careful. The Commanding Officer would expect a satisfactory report. And there was Allan Gerard listening and smiling to himself.

'I think we can settle our differences over a tankard of ale, don't you?'

'No, sir.'

Spanish whispered, 'Try rum.'

'Rum, then.'

'Get out and leave me alone, both of you.'

The soldier looked round the room a little helplessly as though to say, 'You see my difficulties?' but nobody spoke. The men at the table watched him without enmity and without sympathy. Against the wall in the darkness there was a man writing at the desk looking at him speculatively, and a dusty-eyed deer gazed sourly across the room from the wall above. Spanish sniffed and fidgeted his feet as if they were cold, which indeed they were, and hunched his shoulders and rammed his hands more deeply than ever into his pockets and wished earnestly that somebody would say something to ease this deadlock, which he felt to be of his making. He should not have brought the Adjutant here at all. He should have held aloof from the whole affair, except for his ultimate dispensation of official justice as Harbour Commissioner, by letter. He felt his position keenly. And then the Company Commander looked at Alexander Perry and said, 'Now is your chance, Mr. Perry.'

'Mr. Perry,' he told the Adjutant gravely, 'sells lucky charms.'

Coughing a little, fumbling in the pockets of his waist-coat, Alexander Perry came towards the group at the fire. 'Yes,' he said, 'they're good ones too. Very lucky. An essential weapon, if I may so put it, in every soldier's personal armoury.' He extended the small black object on the palm of his hand. 'Have one.'

'No, thank you.'

'Please. Just a sample.'

'What is it?'

'This one is a mountain goat. Found in Thibet: notice the long horns. Keep it. There's no charge.'

Anxious lest he offend the local opinion, of whose support he felt he was going to be much in need, the Adjutant hesitated. They were disinterested now, perhaps unfriendly, but not directly against him. To cause needless offence would do no good at all. And Alexander Perry, sensitive to the soldier's doubt, took the gloved hand and put the charm

in it. 'There,' he said, 'you won't regret it, sir. You will see.'
He nodded and turned back to his desk.

And the Company Commander said sardonically to the
Adjutant,

'Now try.'

The ceiling shook again as somebody you would guess to
be uncomonly heavy walked across the floor above and a
scrap of plaster fell to the floor in the corner near the window and exploded as it struck the linoleum, and they all
listened as though it was for that purpose and reason they
were silent.

'Somebody moving about upstairs,' the Adjutant remarked.

'My wife,' said Daniel Thwaite. He did not look up. 'A
burly woman.'

Nobody spoke. The mechanic blew smoke up towards the
light and they watched it attentively.

'Well!' The Adjutant's voice was unnaturally loud. 'I see
it's a waste of time talking to you now. The naval authorities ——"

'Those bastards!'

'I say the naval authorities ——'

'Not even a pop-gun,' the old man shouted. His voice
cracked suddenly and he began to cough. 'They've given
me nothing,' he cried, choking, 'nothing.' Other ships, he
said, had pop-guns, hadn't they? Hadn't they, Spanish?
Spanish said they certainly had. 'Though I don't think
much to them meself.' He rubbed his chin. 'Sawn-off
barrels, they have, no range.'

'I'll call in the morning,' the Adjutant suggested.

'Afternoon,' Spanish whispered.

'Afternoon, then.'

'See the Chief Engineer,' Captain Thwaite said. 'And listen. Listen to me.' He pulled himself forward in the chair. 'If I catch another of these filthy louts aboard my ship, I'm telling you, I'll throw him into the sea, never mind his blasted barrow. D'y'see?' Keeping his eyes on the soldier, he struck a match and raised his pipe. 'D'y'see?' The match went out.

Hilda Thwaite came into the room and, closing the door, stood there for a moment surprised, her fingers still on the handle, for she was taken aback to find so many in the room, where usually there would be only the old man, her husband, and Spanish maybe, and one or two playing dominoes; sometimes there would be a fisherman, inarticulate and reserved, or a soldier. Her eyes moved from Alexander Perry to Spanish and from them to the players looking at her vacantly and then to the officers; one she knew, and hated, for the mockery that was always in his eyes. The other was strange. He looked fine with his long greatcoat and cap and shining buttons and one thing or another and her hand strayed to the hair on her neck. A smile lit on her lips.

'I'm Mrs. Thwaite,' she said, smiling.

The Adjutant moved uneasily and said he had been talking to her husband, and she laughed a little, fondly. 'He's not well, poor old man,' she said. With the heels of her slippers tapping on the floor she went to the sailor and set the cap straight on his head. 'That's better,' she said, 'that's better.' He did not move at all, sitting rigidly under the hand she laid on his shoulder. 'It's time you were in bed now, Daniel. Come along. Time for bed.' Now she looked at Allan Gerard and what she saw in his eyes could not have pleased her greatly, for it wiped the smile from her mouth as surely as a blow and, momentarily, the brittle serenity from her manner. She did not look at him again.

'Daniel,' she said, 'you've been drinking that nasty rum again.' She took the glass from the arm of his chair. 'You know what I told you.' They watched, fascinated, and she smiled up at the Adjutant. 'He's not well.'

'My God, 'tis the army itself.' O'Hara leaned through the hatch in the wall. 'What's been goin' on in here?' he demanded. 'The very minute me back's turned, somethin' happens. Will you be having a drink, sir?'

'No.'

'You'll be settlin' your troubles, I take it?'

'Shortly.'

Captain Thwaite said aloud, 'Hilda, tell him to give me a drink.'

WHEN the Adjutant had gone. Allan Gerard went to see the guard. He walked down to the railway on the quayside, shortening his stride to meet the sleepers as he turned towards the jetty. He lit a cigarette and the flare of the match in the dark blinded him momentarily and he stumbled. A man cried Halt! coming up at him out of the shadows, visible only against the faint pallor of the sky and peering into his face, bayonet advanced like a feeler worn smooth and gleaming. It was the Company Commander, Allan Gerard said, and the man dropped the point of his weapon and said, Pass, friend, and stood aside, his breath smelling slightly in the cold air. The officer went on to the guardhouse, and past it. The sea moved sonorously among the girders below and to his left the great bulk of the ship loomed against the stars, and, pausing there to read the name on the prow, barely visible, he heard the slow unidentifiable crepitus of the straining beams as she rose to the swell. At the end of the jetty where it was concreted the sea was very close and came swilling noisily over the edge and the wind was stronger; sparks flew from the end of his cigarette. The second sentry halted him there.

The Company Commander said, 'Good evening, Elwes.'

'Good evening, sir.'

'Everything all right?'

'Yes, sir.'

They climbed on to the parapet and leaned against the rail together and listened to the ugly clamour of the sea all round them. On the beach there were men and women moving about the cobles with the stealthiness of shadows on the grey sand, for, though they were not far away, you could hear nothing of their movements. Later, in the early hours of the morning, they would put to sea. The women would gather about the wheels while the men took the weight of the boats on their shoulders and together they would walk the cradles down to the sea and into the surf till the boats were afloat and shying like horses to the waves, leaving the cradles for the women, hip deep with skirts billowing round them on the water, to tow slowly over the shingle. In each boat the last man would shove and then leap for the gunwale, poised there on his knees for a moment while the engines broke into song and roared and settled to a steady hum as the cobles gathered way, heading for the open sea. On the beach in a small crowd the women would watch them, arms akimbo and sodden skirts clinging to their broad thighs in the wind, catching now and then a glimpse of the boats outlined on the crest of a wave against the dawn, climbing up and up and pausing there before the plunge, till they were at one with the sea and indistinguishable from it. Then the women would turn and go home.

The Company Commander said to the sentry, 'Feels like snow, doesn't it?'

'Yes, sir, it does that.'

'Caught any fish recently?'

'No, sir, not since last Tuesday. It's the bait we can't get.'

'How's that?'

'Well, sir, it's the tide. We dig for worms in the sand at low tide. The tides are exceptionally high these days for some reason or other.

'Won't ordinary worms do?'

'Oh, no, sir; the fish don't like them.'

The sea slipped over the edge of the parapet and ran smoothly across the concrete.

'The fishermen give us a bit of fish now and then,' the soldier said.

'That's very decent of them.'

'They're natural-born gentlemen, sir, the fishermen. I don't know how they manage it. They have a hard time of it, what with one thing or another, making ends meet.'

'What's to be done about them, Elwes?' The soldier did not reply at once. 'Or are you going to leave it at that?'

'It's a problem, sir.' He felt he was being drawn into an expression of his own personality, but with the Company Commander you did not protest. 'I know things aren't right, but it's hard to see the cause. Can I offer you a toffee, sir?' He extended a hand in which a few wrapped toffees lay. 'Excuse my fingers, sir.'

'Thank you.' He took one and put it in his mouth. 'Have you been playing your violin any more recently? Where is it?'

'Oh, I don't carry it with me, sir. The other chaps would think it a bit funny, me with a violin. It might get knocked about, too.'

'How would it be if you left it in my office?'

Elwes said, 'That's very kind of you, sir. I don't know when I'd get the time. Or the place, for that matter.'

'Don't you know any of the local fishermen, the chaps who live in the cottages round here?'

'Yes, I do, sir, and very kind they are. As a matter of fact I've had some very pleasant conversational evenings with them. I take a bit of food and they boil it up, you know.' He was quiet for a time, listening to the sea. 'I wish we could do summat for folk like that. I mean all such people. Things aren't good enough, sir, to my way of thinking. Excuse me speaking like this, sir,'

'Go on, go on.'

'I don't know what the answer is, though. Do you sir?'

'Elwes, would I be here if I did? Or you?'

'I suppose not, sir.'

In a moment Allan Gerard said, 'I used to do a bit of writing myself. I was a journalist. Not a very good one, however. I didn't always write what I was told to write.'

Elwes was surprised. 'I never pictured you writing, sir.'

'Didn't you?'

'I thought you'd always been in the army.'

'God forfend.'

The soldier laughed in the dark. Then they were silent for a long time.

'By the way, Elwes,' Gerard said at last, 'I want you to tell Corporal Foster that nobody—nobody, you understand? — is to go on board the blockship from the guard, without my knowledge.'

'Yes, sir. Is there trouble, sir?'

'There may be. Keep clear of it. Tell Foster I said so.'

'Yes, sir. I hope it's nothing serious.'

'I'm afraid there's going to be trouble. You fellows steer clear of it.'

They talked for a little while.

When the Company Commander passed the ship on the

way back, he heard singing. The strange incoherent sound came from all over the ship at once, not from any particular part. Distantly the whole ship sang. It would be the Chief Engineer, Allan Gerard supposed, who was on strike in the engine-room. Smoke drifted across the jetty from the funnel and he caught its acrid stench in the dark.

THE parlour was quiet, Uncle O'Hara served him with a drink and closed the hatch. He stood before the fire and warmed his legs and sipped the whisky. Soon he would go home to the little cottage on the dunes and go to bed and lie awake for a while listening to the sea and the rats in the roof and the wind. The door opened quietly and Hilda Thwaite came in.

'You're back,' she said. She sat down heavily on the arm of the chair and crossed her legs. 'Got a cigarette?'

He offered her his case and lit the cigarette she took.

'I hoped you'd come back,' she said. 'Had enough of Imbleness yet? How long have you been here now? Six months?'

'Approximately.' He watched her face casually.

'Wait till you've been here a year, like me. You wait. A bomber just went over. Very high, it was.'

'I heard it.'

'Wonder if it's German,' she said, scratching one foot with the other, and then, 'Chilblains,' she said — 'I always get them this time of year.'

'Do you now?'

'What were you before the war? I often wondered. I've seen you around a lot.'

'I was a journalist,' Allan Gerard said.

She raised her eyebrows. 'Fancy you. What, newspaper? Fleet Street?'

'I was in Paris, a foreign correspondent.'

'Paris,' she murmured appreciatively.

'Yes.'

She asked him then, 'Why do you drink so much?'

'My father drank.'

She nodded. 'Sort of in the family.'

'Yes,' he agreed gravely, 'we all drink.'

'What are you laughing at?' she demanded suddenly.

'Nothing.' He looked surprised. 'What's the purpose of this visit, Mrs. Thwaite?' he said at length.

'Just social. A girl gets lonely. Cosy in here, isn't it?'

'What is it you want?'

She threw away the cigarette and looked at him. 'What were you looking at me like that for, earlier on, me and Uncle O'Hara? The way you looked.'

'I see.'

'Well, why? You know perfectly well what I mean, don't you?'

'Yes,' he agreed, 'I know what you mean, Mrs. Thwaite. I'll try and explain. I saw something this evening I ought

38

to have seen a long time ago. I hadn't realised it, yet it's been here under my nose for months, the explanation to so many things I haven't understood. It's very interesting. If it were not grotesque, it would be evil.'

She was silent, frowning.

'I don't have to tell you what I mean, Mrs. Thwaite, do I?'

With intervals of mutual revulsion during which they punctiliously ignored one another, she and Uncle O'Hara had been lovers for many months. They could make love only in the afternoons, and this rendered their licence in some way unnatural, maybe that was why they sickened of one another from time to time; for in the afternoons the bar was closed and O'Hara free and Daniel sleeping heavily in the parlour by the fire after the liquor he had taken at midday, and they were not disturbed. Once, unexpectedly, the old man had climbed the stairs and tried the handle of the door, but she had taken care to lock it and did not answer when he called her name; in a few minutes they heard him go down the stairs again, leaning heavily on the banisters. Afterwards, when O'Hara had left her, she would sleep for an hour or two and get up in the early evening with a strand of blonde hair clinging to her face and the imprint of the creases of the pillow bright pink on her moist cheek. She scarcely troubled then to preen herself in the mirror; it was nearly dark, and anyway who was there in Imbleness for whom to make herself beautiful? Except O'Hara? And she was good enough for him as she was; too good, she would tell herself. He made her sick. The beast. She would shiver and make herself a cup of tea on the spirit-stove she kept in the bedroom.

'I don't know what you're getting at, Captain Gerard,' she said slowly.

'Think about it. And let me give you a warning, if I may. Daniel Thwaite is my good friend. In the light of what we both know, I would hesitate to interfere, in your position, with anything to do with the *Ur of the Chaldees*, however remotely or however closely it might seem to affect you personally. Do I make myself clear?'

'No. I don't know what you're talking about.'

'You've done enough harm. Leave the old fellow alone. Anæsthetise him with rum, if you must, but let him run his own ship.'

She shrugged her heavy shoulders. 'What he does with that dirty old barge has nothing to do with me.'

'Fine. Keep on thinking that way. I'm blackmailing you, Mrs. Thwaite, d'you understand?'

'Clever, aren't you?'

He smiled then. 'To tell the truth, I'm a little frightened, but not of you.'

'And suppose I don't ignore what goes on with my husband's ship, what then?'

He said, 'You'd better ask the choirmaster about that.'

Abruptly she stood up. She looked at him with rage and mortification in her eyes, then she went to the door. 'Why do you hate me?' she demanded, turning there. 'I've never done you any harm.'

'My dear woman, I don't hate you. You're trying to build

it up into something taut and emotional. I really don't give a tinker's curse for you either way.'

She went out and slammed the door. He heard the heels of her slippers go up the stairs and tapping and slithering across the floor of the room above.

AND the last was Elwes. He leaned his rifle and bayonet against the chair and eased the helmet back from his forehead where it left a red weal, and bent to warm his hands at the ashes. He had come, he told himself, to get warm after his duty and before going to bed. This he often did. He did not hear the girl come into the room.

It was Agnes. She stood with arms akimbo. 'Frederick Elwes,' she said, 'I thought you were supposed to be doing sentinel.'

He turned, startled and flushing. 'Agnes. I'm just getting warm, lass.'

'Is that all you came for?' she demanded.

'What else should I come for?'

'Gurt fool,' she said. She examined him with a critical eye. 'Look at you, all twisted at the back.' She rearranged the belt, pushing him about. 'Stand still.'

'I can't very well, while you're pushing me.'

'Don't answer me back,' she told him.

'Oh, never mind about it. It's dark, Agnes. It's all right.'

'A fine soldier you'd make.'

'But I am one.' He was indignant.

'God help England, then.' She stood away from him and

looked at the belt. 'There. You'll have to be doing it your-
self in future. I can't always be fixing you, you know.'
She saw a wrinkle at the front of the ill-fitting greatcoat.
'Hold still. There. Frederick Elwes, how old are you?'

'Twenty-four. I wish you'd stop calling me Frederick.'

'I'll call you what I like. Besides, Fred's very common.
Twenty-four.'

He sighed. 'Being twenty-four is a crime against humanity,' he said.

'Twenty-four. And plays the violin.'

'Sh!' He glanced involuntarily at the door, and lowering
his voice, 'What's wrong with playing the violin anyway?'

'Nowt, lad,' she said. 'It's just funny. You.'

'Everybody says that.'

'Let them,' she said at once. 'If I ever hear them, I'll
kill them. And you too, if you ever stop playing, I'll kill
you.'

'Ee, lass,' he said, surprised at the vehemence with which
she spoke.

'I will,' she said.

'But you said yourself you thought it was funny.'

'That's different, what I think.'

Elwes observed that he did not wholly understand
women. She whispered, 'Oh, Fred . . .'' and then stopped.
She turned away to the fire. 'How long is this going on,
Fred? The war?'

'We've only just begun, Agnes.'

'Why did it happen?'

'I don't know. How should I know? Very few know. It

42

just happened, that's all, to most of us. It's nowt to do with us till they want us to fight.'

'We've no bacon for breakfast tomorrow.'

'There's people losing more than bacon.'

She turned to him, her voice strained. 'It's time you were in bed, Frederick Elwes.'

'I suppose so. You seem anxious to get rid of me, Agnes. One of these traveller chaps, is it?'

She threatened to box his ears. 'Traveller chaps! Yes, it is. He's tall and handsome and strong. . . . Go on with you now; I can't tolerate fools. And mind out for that ship; they've been talking about it in here tonight.' She began to shepherd him towards the door.

'I'm going, I'm going,' he protested.

'Have you got everything?'

'My rifle.' He picked it up. 'Anyone would think I was going into a battle or summat, the way you fuss, lass. The invasion.'

'And don't fall into the harbour,' she added.

At the door he turned. Close to him, he was surprised that he was so much the taller; he had always thought her to be taller than he was. Her proximity fascinated him.

'Agnes,' he began.

'Yes?'

'I . . .' he could not speak.

'Yes?' Her lips were parted a little.

'That traveller chap . . .'

She pushed him from the room. 'Go on, get out. Go on, now, Frederick Elwes.'

He said he had wanted to make certain, that was all.

When he had gone, she stood in the middle of the room for a long time, not knowing where to go. She went to the fire and knelt and began slowly to rake the coals of the dead fire. The tears ran down her face and hissed gently in the ash.

A bomber passed overhead, flying low.

FROM the window of his office Spanish watched for the arrival of the Adjutant. His breath steamed the window and he beat his arms across his chest and went back to the stove. It would not snow today, he thought; it was too cold for snow. But the sky was leaden. He lit the gas-ring on the desk and put the kettle on.

When the Adjutant arrived he went out to meet the car. 'He id'n come yet,' he told the officer through the open window. 'I told him, but he id'n come yet.'

'Where is he?'

'In bed, I reckon, or was.'

'Damn the man.'

'Shall you wait?'

'Yes.'

They went into the office. The soldier said it was close in the office. 'Something's got to be done about that ship,' he said. He went to the window and stared at the sky. 'The present state of affairs is intolerable.'

Spanish sniffed and rubbed the stubble on his chin. He

opened the stove and looked in at the fire. Then he went
to the gas-ring.

'Intolerable,' the Adjutant said.

'I'm making meself a cup of tea.'

'If the Boche invades now, that ship will be useless. I'm
not blaming anybody; it isn't a question of blame.'

'It's her is at the bottom of it all.'

'Who?'

'The old man's wife.'

'What's she got to do with it?'

'Sending him off his rocker, she is. She's drove him to
drink and won't give him a penny to drink with. Sugar?'

'No.'

'I like a bit of sugar meself.'

The Adjutant lit a cigarette. 'Well, I can't help that. The
blockship as such is a complete farce. Why or how is not
my business, but it's very much my business to get it put
right, and if civility won't do it, there are other ways.' He
surveyed the little room. 'This your office?'

'Aye.'

'Does the guard behave itself?'

'Oh aye, they're good lads.'

'Why the hell isn't the man here?' He moved about the
room. 'Is he a friend of yours?'

'Middling.'

'Without ballast the ship might just as well not be there.
The naval authorities gave their full approval to the idea of
filling the holds with stuff, and every time I send a chap
near the ship the old man heaves him over the side, or the

barrow anyway. He's too drunk to steer the thing himself and won't let anybody else. And there's a Communist in the engine-room.'

'Edwards is all right. He's on strike.'

'Something's got to be done and pretty damn quick.'

'You won't need a spoon.'

'The ship is filthy, filthy.'

Spanish stirred his tea slowly. 'The birds,' he said, 'the gulls.'

The Adjutant sipped his tea. When he had finished he said, 'I can't wait any longer. Come on, we'll go and find him.'

'He'll likely be in bed.'

'Then he'll have to get up.'

'I'll just finish me tea.' He sipped carefully.

Agnes was sweeping the steps when they reached The Navigator. They went in past her, into the bar where Uncle O'Hara was cleaning glasses.

'Captain Thwaite about?' the Adjutant said briskly. The place smelled pungently of stale beer.

O'Hara rested his plump forearms on the counter. 'Now what would the old man be doin' up at this time of night?' he said. 'If it's my advice you want, I'd tell you to come back this afternoon, when he'll be feelin' a little better and a lot sweeter company after his midday meal, consistin' as it does to a considerable extent of rum.'

'Is he up?'

'He is. And gone out. Mrs. Thwaite is up. The pair of them is up. It's a bloody miracle. The lady's eatin' her lovely breakfast this very minute. Will you be havin' a drop of somethin' to warm you now you're here?'

'Where's he gone?'

'He omitted to inform me. But somethin's up. He hasn't been outa bed this time in a year. Somethin's in the wind and he's gone out.'

'God damn the man!' The soldier turned and went out. Spanish shuffled after him. They left the inn and walked across to the railway lines and along them to the jetty. There were pools of water between the sleepers and the wind rippled their surface. Gulls wheeled and cried over the two men, hovering tremulously on the wind and turning their heads from side to side. Smoke swung about the chimney of the guard-hut and beyond the buffers clothes flapped on the line that ran from the hut to the privy, shirts and pants and socks cracking in the wind like broad whips. The steps outside the door of the hut had been freshly whitened and the trampled barbed wire was bright red with new rust. Beyond, the ship moved slowly with the sea.

They went up the gangway on to the deck. The Adjutant halted and held up a finger. 'There's that singing again.' A gull lit on the wall and watched him. 'Edwards,' Spanish said. He peered up at the bridge and thrust his hands into his pockets. 'Edwards singing.' They listened, Spanish waiting patiently for the soldier to lead the way on to the bridge. They went up. The door of the wheelhouse was stiff, and when the Adjutant kicked it vigorously it flew open and struck something and bounced back. It was quite dark inside, the glass outside being thickly streaked with birdlime. 'I brought the Adjutant, Daniel,' Spanish said. They could see the dark bulk of the old man against the windows. Nobody spoke for a moment.

'You'd better get off my ship,' he said, his voice trembling.

'I've said my say.' He struck a match and held it to his pipe, the flame showing his bright eyes fixed on the soldier's face. He was sober.

'Last night ——'

'If any bloody soldier steps aboard my ship he'll get chucked into the sea.' The match shook in his fingers.

'You said that last night.'

'Maybe.'

'Captain Thwaite, you know as well as I do that as a blockship this ship is useless without ballast.'

'Get another. You won't fill my ship with rubble.'

'It has the full support of the naval authorities.'

The old man took his pipe from his mouth. 'They can kiss my arse,' he said.

'I see.' The soldier drew a breath. 'Just bloody-mindedness.'

'Leave my ship.'

'This isn't my idea, you know. I'm only obeying orders. You seem to think it's all my idea.' Gulls cried outside the windows and the ship heaved with the swell. 'I'll see my Commanding Officer.'

'To hell with the lot of you.'

'Very well.'

Spanish said, 'I told him, Daniel, I told him that's what

you'd say,' and hurried after the Adjutant down the ladder to the deck and the jetty. In his mind the Adjutant was already running over the report he must make to the Commanding Officer. The old man is a danger, he would say, he has a bee in his bonnet. There's no moving him. And the Commanding Officer would smile a little sadly and say, 'What did you expect, Billy?' He would want to know why tact had not been used. 'It seems to me, Billy,' he would say gently, 'that you have made a catastrophic mess of the whole affair. They have made a fool of you. Did you not point out that defence of the country comes above personal considerations?' 'Yes, sir. May I suggest, sir, that steps be taken to remove the old man from the ship?' And the Commanding Officer would say 'Try and remove me from my battalion,' in his quiet voice. He would send for Captain Gerard, the Company Commander, and instruct him to approach the sailor, and the Adjutant would look a damneder fool than ever because Gerard was a civilian soldier and it would put the Adjutant in a difficult position; he was responsible for discipline among the officers. He thought maybe he would go and see Gerard himself and persuade him to see the old man on his own account.

When they reached the guard-hut he told Spanish he would call and see him again shortly. The Harbour Commissioner nodded and shuffled away down the quayside to his office to make some more tea. The Adjutant went into the hut.

Corporal Foster stood up.

'Where's the rest of the guard?'

'One on duty, sir, three on coal fatigue, and Elwes and Simpson here, sir.'

'I see. Has Captain Gerard been in this morning?'

'No, sir.'

'Aren't you the man I spoke to yesterday?' he said to Elwes.

'Yes, sir.'

'Stand to attention, man. What are you doing? Haven't you anything to do?'

Corporal Foster interrupted, 'He's just come off duty, sir.'

'Then he should be getting on with something, Corporal. Sitting on your backside won't win the war, will it?' he asked Elwes.

'No, sir,' said Elwes, swallowing.

'Well, then.'

He turned and went out and Foster said aloud, 'The bastard,' because he liked Elwes. All the guard liked Elwes; they looked after him. He was not complicated; he was like a child and he was a lovely shot with a rifle. Once he brought down a seagull in flight with a Lee-Enfield at nearly a hundred yards; he did not speak to anybody afterwards for a long time. There was something in him that they did not understand, but it was of no importance to them, it was his business. They asked no questions.

The Adjutant got into his truck and directed the driver to Captain Gerard's office on the dunes to the north.

In the streets of the town the quietness was unnatural, the quietness of the young men being away and the fishermen on the sea and the old men standing at the corners in twos and threes waiting, but alone and in silence, and nobody in those shops whose windows were not yet boarded, and they were few, and of the women washing clothes to hang in the yards in the wind with wet red hands and of the expectation of snow or maybe only rain from the quilted sky. There was a train at the station; you could see the white steam distantly. The Adjutant's truck went up the High Street to the level crossing.

Allan Gerard was in his office. It was a derelict cottage in the dunes near the coastguard's tower. The men lived in huts which stood under the trees. There were three huts and each one stood under its own tree, for there were only three of these also, just below the dunes. The huts had double walls, two layers of corrugated iron with a gap of two or three inches between in which the rats ran squealing noisily with their tails rattling on the iron from one end to the other. But the Company Commander lived in the little house. The walls were green with damp and the rats in the roof were very numerous.

The marsh lay to the north, and in the dusk the duck would come in over the old sea-wall flying very high across the moon, but you could hear them muttering among themselves in the empty sky. A patrol went out each night along the sea-wall as far as the battery of six-pounders whose traverse covered only the southern reaches of the marsh, and the gunners there would have tea ready for the patrol in a big enamel jug whose handle was sticky with sugar and anyway too hot to hold. The duck kept their formation beautifully, rather better, the Company Commander thought, than the patrol. Many times he went out in the evening to shoot one, but either they flew too high or the curlew that followed him all the way along the sea-wall from the point where it left the mainland would warn them of the soldier's presence with its mournful cry and they would swerve away to the north. One day, Allan Gerard said, he would get that curlew, but he never did. Later he came to value its company in the lonely marsh and looked out for it. But at dawn as the duck went out they flew low generally, and one morning he got one all right: the leader.

It tumbled out of the sky steeply into the mist that lay maybe two feet deep over the marsh from the dry land to the sea, which at this place was as far away as a mile, and he lost it among the gullies and rivulets. For nearly an hour he waded through the mist with the curlew, hovering over him always a little way behind, crying monotonously and did not find the dead bird until the red sun rose and the mist lifted. It was buried in the mud, having fallen into the bank of one of the many rivulets, and he had to wade through three feet of water, whose brittle crust of ice creaked and snapped against his belly, to reach it. It was a fine bird, a mallard. And there were seals on the beach beyond the marsh; you could see them through the telescope in the coastguard's eyrie that stood on poles like stilts in the dunes, and they would stalk the seals on hands and knees across the frozen sand with Lee-Enfields, but they would never let anyone get close enough for more than a pot-shot at six or seven hundred yards. They were very shy indeed. Allan Gerard used to like to think that he did not try very hard to kill one; they were pretty creatures and the stalking alone was enough. Ostensibly he wanted the pelt to make a jacket, but Nicholls, who was the Bren gunner in number four section and who had been a leather tanner by profession, assured the Company Commander that the skin was no good for that purpose, or any other.

It was frightfully cold on the beach, even though he put on all the clothes he had. It was especially cold at this place, because the tide came in to the wire only with the new moon, and the sea, being so far away that except on the flow it was out of sight, would seep into the sand and this would freeze till the beach was like a glacier off which the wind came viciously, shoving the dunes into little waves whose crests were whipped away in a crazy flurry of sand and sometimes hard dry snow, exposing the mines there and drifting over the flotsam the men had collected and bundles of Chinese currency and oars and broken boxes with the name of a ship on them and pieces of aircraft and one thing or another.

Imbleness was four miles away through the dunes. The country behind was flat, so that you could see the people coming, and if you did not want to talk to them you could go on a tour of inspection of the guns in the pits. They were Vickers and needed a good deal of attention, the barrels corroding quickly in the salty air, so you always had a good reason for not being there. But this time, when the Company Commander saw the Adjutant's truck in the distance, he waited. He stood in the doorway of the cottage. The wind stirred the dune grass and blew the sand into his face.

'Morning, Gerard.'

'Morning, Billy. Long way from home, aren't you?'

'Yes.' The Adjutant seemed uncomfortable.

'Come on in.'

They went into the cottage.

'About the blockship.'

'The old crate in the harbour.'

'The C.O. says something must be done about it. You heard what went on last night. The thing's impossible.'

'No use talking to me about it, Billy. You'd better see old Thwaite; he's the chap. If I put men on that ship again there'll be trouble. He'll shoot the lot.'

'I'm not going to be intimidated by any bloody civilian.'

Allan Gerard smiled. And the smile enraged the Adjutant, as indeed it always did. There was humility in it and mockery and a refusal to be provoked.

'You've got to talk to him, Gerard. You know him; he knows you. He's got to be talked round.'

'Me?'

'Yes. I've tried. Twice now. I've just seen him again.'

The Company Commander said, 'My dear Billy, if a man of your experience fails, what prospect of success have I?' and wished at once he had not said it.

The Adjutant flushed. He longed to bring his cane across Gerard's long face. 'Nevertheless, you've got to talk to him,' he said. 'Ply him with rum. Do anything. We must get the holds filled up somehow and the ship cleaned up a bit. She ought to be manned.'

'By whom?'

'Anybody. Somebody. She ought to be defended.'

'My reserve platoon, Billy, is notoriously prone to sea-sickness.'

'We'll have to see. The first thing to do is to get the old man squared.'

'Take it from me, if you try to put men on the ship permanently, he'll blow the whole bloody harbour up.'

'I can't help that.'

'I see.'

'So you'd better talk to him and let me know the results.'

'The trouble is I'm rather on his side.'

'Oh, you are!'

'Yes.'

'Isn't that a little foolish of you?' He searched Gerard's face.

'Maybe it is.'

'See him today, just the same.'

'Oh, sure.'

'How are the puppies?'

Gerard said they were all right. There was a bitch and four puppies in a basket in the corner of the little room. The Adjutant watched them for a minute in silence.

'Extraordinary,' he said at length. 'Are you married?'

'No.'

'Nor am I.' He went to the door and looked out across

the dunes. 'Don't you ever get sick of these dunes?'

'No, I like them.'

'By the way, that guard of yours on the quay. I don't think much about them.'

'What's the matter with them?' They stood in the sand outside the door of the cottage.

'That boy Elwes is half-witted. He's useless.'

'I don't agree. To begin with, he's the best shot in the company, probably the best in the battalion.'

'That's not everything, not by any means.'

'He also plays the violin very beautifully.'

The Adjutant frowned. 'Neurotic,' he said.

'You know, Billy,' said Gerard, 'whenever I talk to you, sooner or later I want to shoot myself.'

'Oh, why?' The Adjutant looked at him in surprise.

'Let's not pursue the idea.' He was angry with himself.

The Adjutant got into his truck and drove away. In the town he saw Hilda Thwaite. He thought about her all the way back.

SHE left the old man sitting by the fire and went up to her bedroom, to sleep, she said. O'Hara had closed the bar and was washing the glasses there. He was not alone, for you could hear his stridulous voice above the weary rattle of the windows and the murmur of the sea and the cries of the gulls wheeling over the garbage in the yard. The sailor stared at the fire, shifting the cap on his head from time to time and whispering fiercely to himself. He was a little drunk, O'Hara having served him most generously at midday, and his thoughts had neither coherence nor cunning, only defiance.

Captain Thwaite was a simple man, unaware of duplicity. He saw others and what they said and did much as they might wish. But simplicity, perhaps because it is unexpected, has sometimes the manner of great cunning and his reactions had a breathless violence that surprised you. Hilda had been caught by them. She feared his simplicity, not understanding it, and in fact always feared it, since the early days of their marriage, the brutish days when he would return from a long voyage and bed her unsubtly and thereafter accept without question her account of her activities during his absence. He did not ask for the account, nor did he comment. He believed too easily, it seemed to her, and she suspected it, feeling herself led into deep water and there made foolish. He was wholly unconscious of this trifling power he had over her and would not have wished to use it had he known. But she resented it. Even her vindictive attempts to humiliate him bounced back at her, for, having no pride, he was unaware of humiliation. So she nursed her promiscuity as an ace she had never played, growing somewhat careless with the years but never flagrant, anyway in front of Daniel, believing he knew nothing and finding pleasure in this alone. In her own time she would tell him, deliberately, at the right moment. Sometimes she was tempted to tell him, especially when he went to sea, for she was a little jealous of his love of the sea and of the ships he sailed in, not because she wanted his love, indeed the notion was absurd, but rather because she resented his escape; but she said nothing. Then the owners transferred him from the trans-oceanic to the coastal service. He was an old man, they said. He protested violently, but they held to their decision and gave him command of the *Ur of the Chaldees.* He began to drink heavily. He was at home in Newcastle more often and for longer periods and Hilda Thwaite's influence over him increased accordingly. She found that when he was drunk he was more docile than when sober, so she permitted him to drink and even encouraged it, giving him a liberal weekly allowance from the salary he earned and paid immediately to her. When the war broke out he was instructed by the owners to proceed at once to Imbleness, pay off all the crew except the Chief Engineer, and place himself and the ship at the disposal of the Naval Officer in charge of that coastal area. Anticipating conversion to minelayer or maybe even some sort of coastal patrol work, he obeyed the instructions promptly enough. When the N.O.I.C. informed him more fully of his negligible duties, he did not at first understand.

'Your ship is due for breaking up, Captain,' the polite naval officer said, 'so the owners inform me. Nineteen hundred and three, that's getting on for forty years. She's had a good life. Exactly what is wanted for the job. No use for anything else, ideal as a blockship, don't you think? She won't be wasted.'

Captain Thwaite stared at him.

'Coffee?' said the polite naval officer.

'What?'

'I said would you care for some coffee?'

'No.'

'Right, then.'

'I don't understand you. I don't understand any of it.'

'It's all perfectly clear, I think. Your owners ——'

'To hell with the owners. You explain. What happens to me?'

'You will naturally continue to skipper your ship. The owners have given you a splendid chit, Captain. Splendid. Were it not for that, your age ——'

'You're beaching me, is that it?'

'The owners have satisfied us that you are quite capable of doing this important job.'

'Please answer my question.'

'We all have a job to do, Captain Thwaite — if not at sea, then ashore. We are at war, you know.'

'Why am I being beached?'

'You were in all probability sailing ships before I could rock my own cradle. I'm aware of that. Nevertheless I have to inform you that you will take up your duties at Imbleness in three days from now. If you have any difficulty, get in touch with me right away.'

'What am I supposed to be too old for?'

'Should you refuse the job, there are plenty of other men.'

'You're bloody smooth, mister,' said Captain Thwaite.

'My dear man ——'

'I think it's a lot of damned nonsense. The Germans wouldn't take Imbleness harbour if you gave it to them.'

'We have to prepare for all eventualities.'

'Backsides.'

'The military authorities will also co-operate with you. And the Harbour Commissioner, a fellow called Spanish.'

'Is my ship to be armed?'

The polite naval officer said they had only a few old six-pounder available and insufficient ammunition for those. 'Later, perhaps.'

'What the hell am I supposed to do if I'm attacked?'

'Allow yourself to be shelled or rammed and sunk across the harbour mouth.'

'Not even a gun, hey?'

'Not at present. The possibility of filling your ship with concrete will be raised later.'

'Concrete?'

'Ballast of some kind. Bricks, perhaps.'

Captain Thwaite looked at him from under his bushy white brows. ' I don't understand,' he said at length. In a minute he got up and went out.

And for a year the old ship lay against the southern jetty in the harbour at Imbleness and weed grew like yellow hair on her keel and the barnacles showed white on her screw when the water was clear. Rats infested her from stem to stern and the gulls covered her with lime until she stank in the summer sun and her boards warped and sprang. During the first five weeks Captain Thwaite and the Chief Engineer lived on board, the tradesmen of Imbleness delivering groceries to the galley every day. The old man and the engineer cooked it themselves and discussed political science and kept the pressure high in the boilers and drank rum and sometimes whisky, till Captain Thwaite developed a disorder of the stomach and moved to The Navigator, where Hilda presently joined him from Newcastle. The Chief Engineer struck and refused to go ashore in any circumstances, composing a written protest which Daniel nailed to the wall of the saloon bar in The Navigator, where it attracted a good deal of interest at first; Uncle O'Hara raised no objection, since it brought him a wave of extra business. The protest read as follows:

DECLARATION OF STRIKE

I, Andrew Edwards, Chief Engineer of s.s. *Ur of the Chaldees,* do hereby declare a strike against:

1. The owners of this ship on account of marooning Captain Thwaite, master, and me under Admiralty orders and leaving the aforementioned to rot in Imbleness for no adequate reason as can be seen.
2. Also the Admiralty for the manner it's treated experienced sailors and the condition of these turbines which would be overhauled but for the Admiralty.
3. In conclusion, I strike against damfoolery and injustice generally as it is rife especially ashore and refuse to come up till the matter is properly cleared up.

After a time the interest waned, but nobody bothered to take it down and it became stained with beer and flyblown like the rest of the wall.

Hilda Thwaite was not unhappy. She learned to administer rum to the old man, through O'Hara, as an anæsthetist administers ether to a patient, with care and exactitude, so that while he was never wholly incapable, he was seldom sober. Always he wanted more than she allowed him to have, and so her influence was maintained and she could afford to tolerate his preoccupation with the fate of his ship. She let him brood on it, glad that he had something to keep him busy, watching his defiance of the military authorities with a contemptuous disinterest.

He fell asleep. When O'Hara had finished washing the glasses, he went into the parlour quietly and looked at the old man. Then he went upstairs on his toes. The door of Hilda Thwaite's room was open a little and he went in and closed it behind him. The old man was asleep, he said. The floor creaked under his weight, and beneath, the sailor slept.

He was still asleep when Captain Gerard arrived.

'Asleep, Dan?'

He came-to slowly, opening his eyes and peering at the soldier. He saw the uniform. 'You get out,' he muttered.

'It's me, Allan Gerard.'

The sailor cleared his throat. 'Get out, just the same. You're all alike.'

Gerard sat down opposite him. 'You had quite a field day yesterday afternoon, Dan, hadn't you?' He added, 'I only wish I'd been there.'

'Why?'

'I'd have stopped you doing what you did.'

'You wouldn't.' His voice rose. 'They tried. Kicked them off, I did, and will again, if they set foot on my ship, barrows and all.'

'I shall have to pay for that barrow you threw overboard,' he said. 'Did you know?'

The old man frowned. 'You? Why you?'

'I'm financially responsible for every item of equipment in my charge. That's the law in the Army. Don't worry about it, however. If you enjoyed it, splendid! I don't like to see you make a fool of yourself, though, Dan, and by God, you did. It didn't do any good, you know. It was magnificent, but it did nothing but harm. Why did you do it?'

'I had to do something, Allan, lad. Couldn't stand there and watch it without doing something. That's my ship. She got a U-boat in the last war,' he added irrelevantly.

What the sailor had done, Allan Gerard told him, was wild and dangerous and provocative. 'You can't do things that way, Dan. You're not strong enough. They're very powerful. No man alone is good enough. In any case, that's not the way to fight them.'

'Were they your men I kicked off the ship?'

Yes, they were Allan Gerard's men.

'All from that infernal company of yours?'

'Yes, my men.'

The sailor looked at the fire. 'I'm sorry they were yours.'

'That's not the point. That doesn't worry me, or them.'

'Were they under your orders?'

'Of course they're under my orders.'

'Who told them to board my ship in my absence? You?'

Gerard said, 'They're under my orders.'

'Was it that Adjutant fellow?'

Allan Gerard said it was of no consequence where the orders came from. 'To take the law into your own hands like that was arrant idiocy and it's going to cause a great deal of trouble. Why the hell didn't you send for me when you saw soldiers on board?'

'You keep out of it.'

'Dan, we're going to fall out over this.'

'No need,' Captain Thwaite answered simply. 'Just you keep right out of it.'

'I'm for you, not against, man.'

'I'll manage alone.' He put his pipe into his mouth and drew on it, but it was empty. He removed it again. 'You and me have been friends a long time, since you came marching into this town with that company you're so damned proud of. Let's stay friends. I've had enough of being buggered about with, that's all. Don't fight me, lad; I'm a bad-tempered man and somebody might suffer.'

'I'm afraid my men might become involved in some way.'

'Then tell them to stay away from the ship; they'll be all right. They're good enough lads. I hope I didn't hurt any of them yesterday. Nothing personal, tell them.'

Gerard lit a cigarette. 'Do you know, by the way, that it's being suggested a platoon of soldiers he put on board your ship? I mean, permanently?'

He waited, but the storm he had expected did not break.

64

He looked at Captain Thwaite; the sailor was staring at him.

'Soldiers?' he said. 'What for?' And then, 'Who said so?'

'The Army, I suppose. The military authorities. The great They. To scrub the decks, I have no doubt. That's the sort of thing we do mostly; dig holes in the sand and keep the place clean.'

The sailor shook his head in his bewilderment. 'Soldiers?' he said — 'soldiers?' He repeated it to himself, thinking about it.

'If I were you, Dan, I'd sooner have rubble dropped into the holds of my ship than my number fourteen platoon. Sergeant Barnaby is the worst N.C.O. in the whole battalion. He's having a little domestic trouble just now, but he's awful nevertheless.'

And then Elwes opened fire on the mine and the excited clamour burst into the parlour, where the two men fell silent and Captain Thwaite muttered What's that?, and upstairs in the room above Uncle O'Hara raised his glistening head, saying Holy Mother, and Hilda's face turned grey. Above the ship the gulls fled screaming towards the dark low clouds from which the angry noise recoiled like laughter and bounced again and again till you could scarcely tell the noise from the echo. In the High Street Mark Ramsden came out of his shop with Mrs. Fauldes, whom he had been serving, and Ernest Barret came out and the others into the street, and passers-by stopped and turned with maybe one foot on the sidewalk and the other in the road and looked down towards the harbour. Nobody spoke. The noise went booming up the hill and down the streets on either side to

the left and right into every house and room, waking those
who slept in the afternoon and arresting those who were
making tea or baking bread or writing to sons or lovers or
husbands and startling the verger, who was dusting the
organ for this evening's choir practice. In the school below
the station the children, who were singing blithely in con-
cert, wavered and stopped. Mary West, whose husband was
on the sea in a small boat, raised her head with one hand in
the sack of mussels she was shelling for baiting the hooks
tonight and listened, the wind moving her long hair gently.
The noise went up over the crest of the hill beyond the
reservoir. It was the guard, Mark Ramsden called across the
street, and Gilderson said he expected they were firing at
a mine or something, and Miss Honeyman said it was those
silly soldiers again who had nothing better to do than
frighten folk, as if the war were not enough. And everybody
relaxed a little and moved about with exaggerated non-
chalance, pleased that the war had come so close and found
them unmoved by its proximity.

On the jetty Corporal Foster told Elwes to raise the
sights fifty yards, that he was firing low, and Elwes adjusted
the sights and fired again. With binoculars Corporal Foster
watched the splashing of the bullets where they hit the
water round the black thing in the water going south with
the drift. He thought it was maybe six hundred yards away.

'Fresh magazine,' Elwes said.

Corporal Foster smartly replaced the empty magazine
with a full one. When you were as close to the gun as that
its frantic stutter drummed heavily on your ears, but when

you were firing you didn't notice it; you got very angry with the way your body shook and the tripod legs shifted over the smooth concrete with the vibration. The empty cases tinkled sweetly on the jetty and a few rolled over into the sea. Then there was a small boat on the crest of a wave near the mine, and when Corporal Foster saw it he shouted and Elwes raised his head and stopped firing. It was a boat, Corporal Foster said. He was alarmed. The boat dipped steeply into the trough, and when it reappeared there was a man in it standing up holding on to the tiller in the stern and waving. He was close to the mine, but he had seen it.

The fisherman was Watson West returning with what he had caught. The fish lay in boxes on the bottom of the boat, white bellies upward, dogfish and whiting and codling and skate and a lobster that was still alive. Over the boxes the dabs lay. These were made of pigskin blown up like balloons and had short poles running through them which carried a small flag on one end; you attached the lines to the other end. The dabs floated and marked the position of the lines and were tethered by them, for the lines lay on the sea bed. Watson West had heard the bullets whispering over his head and had seen the little splashes in the sea where they struck. Once or twice a ricochet had whined over the bows of his coble and far into the sky, mournfully. He guessed maybe they were shooting at a mine and slowed to half-speed, looking for it. When he saw it, he turned south and skirted it wide; the horns stood up out of the water and there was a white froth round them. Then he headed for the beach. When he had, auctioned the catch he would go home and have very sweet tea and the lobster with his wife and help her to bait the hooks ready for tomorrow. Afterwards he would work a little on the violin. For a long time he had deliberately dawdled in his work on the instrument, because he knew that when it was finished he would have lost something. He had been working on it for three years and eight months. But he could not keep away from it and it was nearly finished. Indeed you could play it now, he thought, but there were still a few things to be done, especially to the bow. He did not know what he would do with it when it was complete. At first, when he had first begun the work, he had decided in his mind that Eunice should learn to play it if it were playable at all; the publishers of the book called *How to Make a Violin,* which he had used and whose instructions he had closely followed, advertised on the last page of the booklet a similar tract called *Now Learn to Play It.* But Eunice was blown up in the minefield on the dunes. He could not play it himself.

Elwes and Corporal Foster watched him sheepishly from the jetty.

Corporal Foster shouted, 'Sorry!' when the coble came level with them. 'We were firing at a mine.'

The fisherman looked up. 'I saw it,' he called. The boat's flat prow struck sharply at the waves swinging from the jetty.

On the beach Mary West and Mrs. Moon and the others who were waiting for the men still at sea and one or two

of those who were already ashore gathered round the cradle
Watson West used and shoved it down to the water's edge,
the trailing shaft leaving a long furrow in the wet sand.
Riding the high surf, Watson West waited till they ran out
the cradle to the boat and then gave it a touch of throttle,
hesitated, and settled gently on the berth. Mary West stood
beside the coble with one hand on the gunwale and looked
up at him, brushing back the hair the wind blew across her
face. She smiled, showing her teeth. The black skirt she
wore ballooned on the surface so that her big white legs
were visible in the water beneath. He climbed out of the
coble and took the weight of the stern on his shoulders.
Then, leaning stiffly on the rope till their feet sank ankle-
deep in the wet sand, they pulled the cradle up the beach.
Gulls gathered over the boat. A few drops of rain fell.
At the head of the beach a little crowd waited with
the baskets for the auction. The Harbour Commissioner
hunched his shoulders and turned up the collar of his coat
against the rain and waited, hoping absently that he did
not appear to wait and was there only in his official capac-
ity; he was waiting for the fish Watson West would give
him presently. Already he had three fish, two codlings and
an eel, in a newspaper under his arm. For the fishermen
gave him a fish every day. It was almost obligatory to give
Spanish a fish. Nobody knew why. He seemed as an official
to expect it. Maybe it would pay some time. In any case,
he gave away most of those he received in this manner, to
Uncle O'Hara or Captain Thwaite or the Corporal of the
guard. Furtively, because it was accepted in the same way,

Watson West gave him a whiting and he wrapped it up in the newspaper with the others. After the auction he walked up the long cobbled slope to The Navigator. At the foot of the stairs in the dark hall of the inn he stoood for a moment listening. When he had heard what he expected to hear, he left the inn and went home. Rain dripped steadily from the peak of his cap.

It did not rain for long. Afterwards the sun broke through and the light was a pale limpid green. Uncle O'Hara set out to take the choir practice at St. Thomas's. He called for the children on the way. Some came unbidden, or, knowing it was time for the choir practice, waited in the street till they saw the big man come round the corner with the other children, and ran to join them. Soon there were many, holding on to his hands and coat, laughing and chattering all the way up the hill.

'I saw Captain Thwaite this morning, sir,' the Adjutant said to the Commanding Officer. 'We shall have to show our horns a bit. The interview was on the stormy side.'

The Commanding Officer said he had expected as much.

'Actually we were thrown off the ship.'

'Bodily?'

'Ordered off,' the Adjutant said. 'No bones about it, though. Pure bloody-mindedness. Made me very cross indeed. I told Gerard to have a go, but I'm afraid it's a waste of time. He simply isn't trained to handle a situation of that sort.'

'As I remember it, Billy, it isn't included in the Sandhurst curriculum either.'

'I quite agree, sir, but Gerard doesn't seem to grasp even the essentials. He doesn't try. Seems to take a pride in his civilian attitude to everything.'

'Billy, it would be as well, I think, if you dropped the notion that all civilians are damned fools by nature. In my experience they're sometimes quite intelligent and nearly always pretty good soldiers. Nor could we win the war without them.'

'They need a lot of teaching, sir, the devil of a lot.'

'Go on about the ship.'

'Yes, sir. I think we shall have to adopt the Brigadier's suggestion and put a platoon on board her. One of Gerard's. I mean billet them there.'

'I don't like the idea at all. I never did.'

'Don't you, sir? I thought it quite a good one.'

'They'd be sick,' the Colonel said, 'all over the place.'

'Not all of them, surely. They'd get used to it. Nelson was as sick as a dog for the first week of every voyage he ever made.'

'Yes, but he was a sailor.'

No, the Adjutant was not amused.

'I mean it wouldn't do the chaps any harm to be sick.'

'Undoubtedly being sick is most desirable, but I still doubt if the men would appreciate it much.'

The Adjutant took off his glasses and cleaned them. Sometimes he did not understand the Commanding Officer.

'Further,' the Colonel continued, 'I think if I were Captain Thwaite I'd hate to have a platoon of soldiers puking all over my ship.'

'They'd clean it up.'

'I'd hate it anyway, whether they were sick or not.'

'Well, sir.'

'You mean that wouldn't matter much, don't you?'

'Sir, the ship is absolutely useless as it is now. It's a liability. It jeopardises the whole of the defence of the harbour. The ship itself is falling to bits, the old man is drunk from morning till night, and the Chief Engineer is a Communist. He won't come up. He ought to be ordered to come up.'

'Why?'

The Adjutant said, 'Well.' He floundered a little. 'Well, sir, d'you think chaps ought to be allowed to say what they will and won't do, like that? With things as they are? It's anarchy, sir. Supposing everyone did it.'

'He's probably very comfortable down there, Billy. Where else should the engineer be?'

That was not the point, the Adjutant said. 'It's the principle.' His hand fluttered about and eventually settled on his moustache. 'The whole affair's tainted with the same sort of thing. Old Thwaite's just as bad. He won't even let us on board now. The naval people think we're crazy.'

'Let them.'

'All we do is argue.'

'It's all most enjoyable.'

'Well, sir,' the Adjutant said again. The Commanding Officer's resilience frequently exasperated the Adjutant. He looked upon it as a weakness. You could not argue with it because it escaped you. Well, sir, the Adjutant would say as though that was the end of it and he had done his best, and then he would sometimes catch a curious light in the Colonel's mild eyes, watching him, and would feel uncomfortable for no adequate reason. There were moments when he hated the Commanding Officer.

But he continued, 'If we put a platoon on board, and I'm sure the naval people would be only too glad to wash their hands of the whole thing — after all it's our responsibility — we could at least be sure the ship was clean. Just now it stinks like an aviary. It would make ideal billets for the men. They could man it, sir. I mean fortify it, mount Brens on the deck and the old Lewis gun. There's a galley which would make an excellent cooking-point. And the men could fill up the holds as arranged. If Thwaite objects, we'd have a useful reason for getting rid of the old mule altogether.'

'Billy, you're a bit of a Fascist — d'you know that?'

The Adjutant shifted uncomfortably. 'We're responsible for the defence of the harbour,' he said doggedly.

'No, Billy,' said the Colonel gently. 'I am.'

The Adjutant stiffened.

'And I don't think the old chap would agree. I wouldn't.'

The Adjutant said, 'No, sir,' and thought to himself maybe that was why the Commanding Officer was only a lieutenant-colonel after twenty-six years' service and maybe if he paid a little more attention to those above him and rather less to those below he might become a brigadier, if he were not already too old. The Adjutant did not propose to make the same mistake. When he looked up the Colonel was watching him.

'Yes,' he said, 'perhaps you're right, Billy.'

The Adjutant flushed. Sometimes the Commanding Officer was wickedly perspicacious.

'Well, Billy?'

'Permission to fall out, sir, please.'

'Go and have your tea. I'll talk to the Brigadier about it all.'

'Thank you, sir.' He added, 'I'll have one more shot at the old man this evening. I'll try a different approach.'

The Commanding Officer said that would be all right and stood up and went to the fire. 'I had a letter from my son this morning,' he said. 'Says he wants to be an architect, of all things.' He took the letter out of his pocket and read it again.

'One of those builder fellows?'

'Apparently.'

'Extraordinary thing.'

'It's probably his mother who's behind it.'

'He'll change his mind, sir.' He saluted and went out, and the Commanding Officer thought for a long time about how his son wanted to be an architect. He read the letter again.

★

THE bar was not open when the Adjutant went back to the inn. He looked in the parlour and saw Captain Thwaite asleep in the chair before the fire and went out again, closing the door gently. In the kitchen he found Agnes and asked to see Mrs. Thwaite, and the girl went upstairs muttering to herself and knocked on the bedroom door. 'There's a man to see you,' she said briefly when Hilda opened it.

'A man? Who?'

'Don't know. An Army officer.' She went downstairs.

Hilda Thwaite took the kettle off the stove on the wash-stand and looked at herself in the mirror and put out her tongue angrily at the face she saw there. She pushed back the heavy fair hair from her eyes. The heels of her slippers tapped on the floor of the landing and the Adjutant, stand-ing at the foot of the stairs, looked up.

'Mrs. Thwaite?'

'Yes, what is it?'

'Can I speak to you alone for a moment?'

She came down the stairs out of the shadow. 'Well?'

'It's about your husband.'

'He's had an accident,' she said at once.

'No.' The Adjutant was surprised. 'He's asleep in the parlour.'

'Come in here.' She led him into the dining-room. 'You gave me quite a fright.'

She sat down and crossed her legs.

'Make yourself comfy. Cold in here, isn't it?' She shivered and drew the skirt down over her knees.

The Adjutant sat down. 'Mrs. Thwaite,' he began, 'are you aware that there's been a certain amount of trouble about your husband's ship?'

'O God, I thought it was something important.'

'It's getting rather serious.'

'Go on, he's only pulling your leg. Don't be so silly.'

The Adjutant moved uneasily. 'The *Ur of the Chaldees*,' he said, 'is supposed to be the blockship for the harbour and stop anything coming in. Your husband is Captain of the ship and we have the impression just now that he's not co-operating as well as he might. He'— the Adjutant hesitated —'he drinks rather a lot, doesn't he?'

'What's that got to do with it?'

'Well, the Brigadier's inclined to take a poor view of it.'

'Tell him to mind his own business, then.'

'Unfortunately it is his business. The thing that's caused the most trouble is that Captain Thwaite won't let us fill the hold of his ship with rubble. Bricks and stuff. Ballast. He refuses to let anybody on board.'

'Can't say I blame him, but go on.'

'The idea now is to put a platoon of soldiers on board to look after things.'

'The cheek!'

'I thought perhaps you'd like to know about it?'

'Why me?' she asked him suspiciously. 'Why should I want to know?'

'Well, it's possible your husband will react impulsively, Mrs. Thwaite. He may do something he'll regret. You might like to discuss it with him. That's all.' She wished she could

see his face. His back was to the light and only his glasses
shone in the dark oval of his head, leaning towards her
now so that she could read into his words only what she
could hear in his voice. 'We're very much opposed to the
naval people taking a hand,' he said, 'or of course the
owners of the ship. Possibly Captain Thwaite will be too.
He's likely to get his pension soon, isn't he?'

She said abruptly, 'They can't touch that.'

'To jeopardise it now after so long seems a pity.'

'The swine!' she said. Now it was clear; she understood
what Allan Gerard had meant.

'They might decide to replace him.'

'The dirty swine! Would you believe it, eh?' Her voice
rose. 'Behind my back.' She stood up.

'He's awfully obstinate.'

'How long's things been like this?'

'Oh, quite a long time. He won't listen to me.'

'He'll listen to me, though.' Her big breasts rose and fell.
'Leave him to me, mister.'

'We really will have to do something about it soon. It's
only a question of moving a handful of men aboard the
ship.'

'By the time I've done with him,' she said, 'he'll let
you put the whole bloody Army on board, and glad to.'

'Thank you, Mrs. Thwaite.'

He left her. She went up the stairs. In the saloon he
found Agnes, who said that the bar was not yet open.
'Choir practice,' she said laconically. He did not understand, but it did not seem important and he left the inn

and drove along the quayside slowly through the pools of rain and up the quiet dark High Street. Beyond the hill there was a little light left in the sky. It caught the white manes of the waves rolling in towards the harbour.

UNCLE O'HARA flung open the hatch in the wall and thrust his shining head into the parlour. 'What's been goin' on in here in me absence?' he demanded. 'There's guilt in the air.'

Captain Thwaite said it was time O'Hara was back. 'Get me a double tot of rum and quick about it.'

'No sooner do I turn me back than it's in trouble you are and excitin' things happening in me own place and me on the Lord's business and deprived of the pleasure of seein' them.'

'Rum, man.'

'Ho'd your whisht, y'ould bilge-rat. Dear, oh dear, you should have heard me this night. In fine voice I was and the darlin' childer aghast at the power of me singin'.' He opened his mouth and sang. 'For all the saints,' he bawled, 'who from their labours rest.' He coughed throatily. 'As fine a bit of Bach as you ever heard, callin' for powerful emotion and gettin' it.' 'To Thee,' he sang, dwelling on the note, ' "by faith," ' the veins on his temples stood out and the polished dome of his head turned slowly purple, ' "before the world confessed." Magnificent.' He added, 'St. Thomas's is in terrible need of a new organist.'

'For the last time, will you get me a rum?'

'Hallelujah,' sang the publican.

The old man was drinking when Hilda Thwaite came in. She took the glass from his hand and placed it on the mantelpiece. That was enough, she said. Her face was white and unpowdered and there was no flamboyance in her manner. The sailor made no effort to hold the glass. He waited then. She stood over him.

'I want to talk to you,' she said, 'upstairs.'

'I'm busy.' He shifted the cap on his head. 'What's it about?'

'Never mind what it's about.'

'I can't come now.'

'Come on.'

'Later.'

'Come on.' Her voice did not change and she laid a hand on his shoulder. 'There's a good boy.'

'I'm not drunk,' he said. 'I haven't had a drink.'

'Are you coming?'

He got to his feet and held on to the mantelpiece.

'There's a good boy.'

'I'm not a boy.'

She laughed a little. 'You men,' she said. 'Boys, that's all you are. Come along.'

She followed him out with her hand on his back, and in the hall he turned and told her to take her hand off his back, petulantly, and she did so. They went up the stairs and into the bedroom, where the bed was unmade and the teapot and cup and saucer stood on the washstand and the bevelling of the mirror reflected the light across the ceiling in curving bars of blue and green and yellow and gaudy red. She thrust the clothes that were on the chair on to the bed and pointed to the chair.

'Sit there.'

He sat down.

'I had a visitor this afternoon,' she began.

He said nothing and she waited for him to speak.

'Well,' she said, 'don't you want to know who it was? Aren't you interested?'

'No,' he answered simply. His eyes strayed to the bed and then fell to the floor.

'It wasn't a man, if that's what you're thinking,' she said bitterly. 'That's what you would think. That's what you would think of your wife — that's typical.'

He said mildly that he had never thought of such a thing; was she not his wife?

'Yes, you did.' With each word she grew angrier that the conversation had not taken the turn she had intended it should take and angry with herself that she was allowing it to happen. 'Never mind who it was came to see me.' She moved about the room with the heels of her slippers tapping loudly on the naked linoleum and under her weight the floor sighed. 'I learned a lot this afternoon.' Her voice rose. 'A lot, Mister Captain Thwaite.' She faced him squarely. 'And I looked a fool not knowing it already, I might add, apart from anything else. Made me look a damned fool. I was ashamed. My own husband. My own husband,' she shouted.

Captain Thwaite said the people next door would hear her. She ought to lower her voice, he said.

'Let them, let them. Let them hear what sort of a drunken sot I've had to spend my life with. I'm forty-one next — d'you know that? Forty-one. And look at me. The best years of my life.' As she moved past the mirror each time she looked at herself and drew in her belly.

'What's the matter, Hilda?' he asked her gently.

She laughed.

'No, don't laugh like that.'

'It's funny,' she said. 'I can't help seeing the funny side.'

He did not speak. She stood with her back to the mirror and the bevel threw red and yellow beams over her thick, fair hair. He watched it absently. He could see the back of her neck in the mirror and the brown hair beneath the tawny hair.

'I could have left you a dozen times. A dozen times I could have had everything I wanted. But I didn't. I didn't, like a fool. I stuck by you.' Her voice rose shrilly. 'And this is what I get for it. Behind my back.'

'I don't understand,' he said heavily. 'I don't know what you're talking about.'

'Liar.' She leaned close over him, so that flecks of spittle struck him in the face with the violence with which she spoke, and he flinched. 'You're a liar. I know now, see? I know all about it. You can't fool me any longer. I was told this afternoon. Never mind who told me. I was told, that's enough.'

'You always must shout.'

'I'll shout my head off. What's been going on with that ship, eh? Behind my back. Don't tell me you don't understand.'

He raised his head and looked at her in astonishment. 'My ship?'

'Yes. The ship out there in the harbour. The blockship. I'm the laughing-stock of the place with it.'

'But it hasn't got anything to do with you.'

She made a gesture of impatience. 'You must think I'm an idiot.'

'No, Hilda; you're a very capable woman,' he said. 'I've always admired you a great deal.'

'Then what do you think is the matter with me? Go on, tell me. I'd like to know. I'm very curious. Tell me what's the matter with me.'

'Well,' he said slowly, 'I've always thought what a pity it was we didn't have any children for one thing.'

She stared at him open-mouthed. Then she threw back her head and laughed suddenly. 'Children!' She slapped her thigh and went off into high-pitched laughter. 'Children! Oh, my God!'

He watched her curiously. 'What are you laughing at?'

'Poor Daniel.'

'I think we were wrong,' he persisted. 'I've always thought so, Hilda. It was a great mistake.'

'You're unbelievable!'

He said nothing, watching her.

'I don't believe it, no!'

'Is it too late?' he asked her in a moment.

Now she stared at him breathless with her small laughter and then began again to laugh, to laugh big, slowly at first and incredulously and then louder and higher. She laughed for a long time. The tears ran down her cheeks and she swayed to and fro, slapping her broad thigh.

'People will hear you, Hilda.' He was very puzzled. 'I'd better go,' he said.

She pushed him back on the chair as he tried to rise and wiped the tears from her cheeks with her fingers. 'Oh no.' She went to the mirror. 'Now I look a sight,' she said.

He waited. 'Is there anything else?'

'I haven't begun.'

He watched her while she looked at herself in the mirror, patting her hair and dabbing at her eyes.

'It was about the ship,' he said tentatively.

She turned now. 'Yes. The Army's going to put some soldiers on the ship.'

'No, Hilda.'

'You've told them you'd chuck them off. I know all about it.'

'I don't see that it has anything to do with you,' he said.

'Don't you? Well, I do. And I'll tell you why. Because you've got responsibilities to me as well as your ship. And I come first. Why should I play second fiddle to that old hulk? Tell me that. Just tell me. Go on, tell me.'

'I won't have soldiers on board my ship.'

'Don't tell me what you will and won't do. I know what the game is.'

He waited for her to go on. 'Well?'

'Don't think you're going to do me out of that pension, because you're not.'

He understood. 'My dear girl,' he began.

'Don't my dear me.' She leaned over him. 'I haven't waited all these years for nothing,' she said. 'You're going to have soldiers on the ship, and like it.'

'What's the pension got to do with it?'

'Suppose they sack you, eh? Because you won't let soldiers on board. What then?'

'Who? Who'll sack me?'

'Oh, stop it now. The Navy. The owners. The military. Anybody.'

'They wouldn't sack me. I've been with them forty years now. They've a lot of faults, but they wouldn't do that. I know them, Hilda.'

'They beached you, didn't they?'

'They wouldn't sack me like that.'

'Such innocence! They'd get rid of you without a thought if they wanted, make no mistake. And then what, eh? Then what about the pension? You hadn't thought of that, had you? Well, think of it. You've a duty to me, and if you don't know that yet I'll soon show you. The pension is mine, you understand. I've waited long enough for it. It's what you owe me, that pension.'

'The pension has nothing to do with it, Hilda.'

'Oh yes, it has. I'm not going to starve. All my life I've been looking forward to that pension.'

'They wouldn't stop the pension. I've always been loyal to them.'

'I'm not taking any risks. You'll tell the Army they can put soldiers on board as soon as they like.'

He shook his head. 'You don't understand.'

'Will you tell them, or shall I?'

'No.' He avoided her eyes.

'What's the matter with having soldiers on board anyway?' But he did not reply. 'You'll tell them tomorrow.'

'You don't know what you're doing,' he muttered. 'You're interfering in something you don't know about, Hilda.'

She said again, 'Is it to be me, or you?'

He drew a deep breath. 'I'll talk to them,' he whispered. 'I'll do it.'

'Tomorrow.'

'Very well, Hilda, tomorrow.'

'I don't trust you,' she said suddenly. Nor did she. It was easier than it should have been.

'I've said I'll talk to them, haven't I? Now be quiet.'

'I think I'll be there,' she said.

'I will do it, alone.'

She nodded. 'All right. And no more rum till you do, not a single drop.'

He did not answer. In a minute he said, 'God alone knows what Edwards will say.'

'Who?'

'Edwards,' he said, 'the Engineer.' His hands moved over his pockets searching for something and found nothing and fell again to his knees. 'You don't know what you're doing. There's a lot of people affected.'

'We'll see.'

He got to his feet with an effort. 'I knew we ought to have had children. I always knew.'

She was at the mirror. 'You make me sick,' she said. He went out, closing the door quietly behind him, and she heard the whistle of his rubber boots going along the corridor to the landing and down the stairs. She powdered her face with a feeling of dissatisfaction. She had not said all she had intended to say and there was something lacking in her success. Usually he fought her and she had to shout him into submission, till he was tired and beaten and she was confident that he would do what she commanded. This time he had acquiesced too easily and something had escaped her. She powdered her frowning face heavily, feeling a little helpless.

The verger and the mechanic from the empty garage in the High Street were playing dominoes at the table under the light when the sailor returned to the parlour. They looked up when he came in and exchanged little smiles.

The sailor replied, 'She doesn't mean harm. She's not happy, that's all.' He felt for his pipe. 'She's a bit lonely, that's all.'

OUTSIDE it had begun to freeze lightly. The moon, which was not yet full, rose yellow over the sea, and when it had risen out of the mist everything in its path glittered softly with the frost, and the crowded white faces of the town looked down to the harbour where the sea ran smoothly along the quay in the shadow, washing the weeds that grew out of the concrete as it rose and fell. The five boats, of which two were waterlogged, moored to the steps below the Harbour Commissioner's office, jostled patiently in the dark and the sea slapped and sucked at their distended flanks. In the guard-house beyond the buffers there was a light below the window, and the shirts hanging on the line to the privy stiffened slowly under the frost, casting long shadows across the pools of rain not yet ice among the clinker on the ground. The ship against the jetty moved unwillingly in the swell and a long way away, on the bridge, a bottle rolled to and fro.

On the jetty the sentries walked up and down to keep warm. They did not talk to one another very much, each having his own thoughts and these were sufficient. At night there are always two sentries. They waited for the reliefs so that they might go to bed. In the hut it would be very warm and dark and smelling of paraffin and sleeping men and damp clothes, and the fumes of the stove would sting their eyes until they were accustomed to it. On the table there was a hurricane-lamp, smoke from whose ragged wick had blackened the upper half of the glass so that the light fell only on to the floor in a circle. There would be somebody snoring in the shadow beyond the table and the others would stir in their sleep. Corporal Foster would be sitting at the table reading; he was a rare one for reading, and smoking, and keeping the tea hot. The enamel jug stood on the stove, hissing a little. A truck went grinding up the hill towards the level crossing; the wisp of sound clung to the quiet streets for a long time after the lights of the vehicle had gone.

Beyond the dunes, to the north, the patrol moved slowly along the sea-wall. In the marsh nothing stirred. They thought of the tea they would drink that the gunners would have ready for them and of the way the frost got into their boots, and watched their shadows cast by the rising moon far over the desolate land moving grotesquely with them. A bird rose whirring at the feet of the Corporal and fled into the night. Nothing else happened.

In the cottage under the dunes the Company Command-er sat alone in front of the small fire and worked. On the table there was a lamp. The rats ran to and fro in the roof and the dog on the floor whimpered in his sleep. The officer was tired and his mind wandered from the thing he was writing. It was curious how your mind moved of its own volition now from the street lamps one after the other shining in through the open window moving across his face and over the drawn blind of the window on the other side of the ambulance along gathering speed to the glass through which he could discern the backside of the driver whose dusty cob lugged him to the fever hospital that night, and going on, without your bidding, to the sudden cold touch of the pearls your mother wore swinging down against your chin when she got on her knees in the dim red firelight to kiss you as you drowsed under the table where your father had carried you sleeping for a little extra protection against the bombs the Zeppelin might drop and did not because afterwards its flaming carcass fell in flames in the sky at Billericay, and taking *Virginibus Puerisque* in his hands from the headmaster saying most politely as he did so, Thank you, sir, but I have read this, which was true if impolitic, and the headmaster giving him *Barchester Towers* instead, irritably, and six Speech Days at which six great statesmen gave him six recipes for success whose common denominator was, generally speaking: Obey. Lying bastards, he thought. And then back to the woman again, always back to her, with his face buried in the wool of the jersey she wore and clinging to the roughness of his chin and her whole body trembling helplessly as his hands moved over her and her fingers fluttered and closed over the back of his head as though they had lost something and now had found it again. His arms tightened about her and his mind soared dizzily among the cold stars.

QUITE early on the following morning the Harbour Commissioner came to the inn. Only Alexander Perry was in the dining-room. He had finished his breakfast. He was smoking. The first cigarette of the day, he said, was always the best. He dusted his waistcoat and sharply, as though coughing, blew ash from the cigarette between his lips. The habit gave him a curious pleasure, he was seldom unconscious of it; indeed, he had sometimes to remind himself that it was in that way that Alexander Perry normally disposed of his

cigarette ash. He examined his card for the day. He had
one such card for each day of the month, showing the day's
calls and what he might reasonably expect to sell at each,
two gross of lucky charms or assorted purses or maybe only
a dozen, with advertising matter for display, and against the
name of each customer he wrote his own notes on the man's
character, some small foible, something he might use in his
approach to the customer, as a means of overcoming what
Mr. Beardwood called Sales Resistance. He knew his cards
by heart, but the system was a good one and it was a pity
not to use it.

Uncle O'Hara entered the room silently on slippered
feet, braces trailing at his heels from his waist and stomach
trenchantly out-thrust. He was polishing a glass.

'How was the lovely breakfast this mornin'?' He breathed
hoarsely into the glass.

'Eminently satisfactory,' Alexander Perry replied. He
belched delicately and adjusted the glasses on his nose.

'That's good. Will you be havin' a look at the mornin'
paper? You'll find it on the table in the tastefully furnished
lounge.' He followed the traveller into the parlour. 'London
got it again last night.'

'So I see.'

And then the old Lewis gun on the jetty opened fire.
The frenzied din was softened a little by distance, but
everything in the room seemed to hold its breath for a
moment and the light trembled. Alexander Perry started to
his feet. He stared at the publican and the trace of colour in
his cheeks left them.

He whispered, 'O God!'

O'Hara did not move. His eyes were fixed on the windows. And the gun fired again, a long, excited burst.

The traveller said, 'Is this it?'

They waited.

'The paper said . . .' There was a film of moisture on his forehead. 'They're here.'

The publican shook his head, listening.

'Listen.'

But there was no more firing then. The traveller took a deep breath in the silence and let it out through parted lips. The publican went to the windows and looked out towards the jetty. While he was there and Alexander Perry watched him, the Harbour Commissioner came in.

'What's the matter?' he said. He also seemed somewhat agitated.

'They've come,' Perry told him. 'They're here.'

'Who?'

'That firing.'

'Well?'

'The invasion. The enemy.'

Spanish said, 'Ey, dear, man, that's nobbut those daft lads on the quayside yonder firing at a mine. There's things more important than that to think about now.'

'Mines? What mines, pray?'

'Them as breaks loose from the minefield yonder. The lads try to set them off as they drift past the jetty. It passes the time for them. They never hit owt.'

O'Hara said, 'They ought to warn people.'

But Spanish only asked him if Captain Thwaite was up yet. Alexander Perry left the room without a word.

'No,' the publican answered, 'he's not. Nor likely to be for some time to come.'

'Then he'll have to get up.'

He went up the dark stairs, muttering anxiously to himself. On the landing he encountered Alexander Perry again. The traveller now was calm. He carried an umbrella and wore a hard black hat and gloves and in his hand there was a revolver and he was loading it.

Spanish looked at the gun. 'What's that?'

'My old service revolver.' He went on loading it, slipping the rounds into the chambers. 'I've always carried it with me, ever since Dunkirk.' It was just as well to be prepared, he said. He went down the stairs slowly, putting the gun into his pocket.

Spanish knew which room was Captain Thwaite's and knocked on the door, and when nobody answered pushed it open gently and switched on the light. The old man was asleep in the bed with his mouth open and Hilda Thwaite lay beside him like a range of hills beneath the blankets.

'Captain Thwaite.' He shook the sleeping sailor. 'Daniel.'

Hilda Thwaite opened her eyes. 'Who is it?'

'Me, ma'am — Spanish.'

'What do you want? Get out. This is a lady's bedroom.'

Spanish took off his cap, the short white hair beneath standing up fiercely as it was released. 'Much obliged,' he said. 'It's the Captain, though.' He shook the old man again.

'What is it?' the woman demanded. She reared up on her elbow. 'What is wrong?'

Spanish told her, 'The Adjutant's coming. And the Brigadier. And the Commanding Officer. Everybody. They're all coming.'

WHEN they arrived, Spanish was waiting on the quayside alone. There were three cars. They drew up in order of seniority outside the Harbour Commissioner's office, and the drivers got out and drifted together and lit cigarettes. The Brigadier was tall and exquisitely dressed; he looked like an advertisement. He was followed by the Commanding Officer, who seemed ill at ease, and by the Brigade Major, who carried a large map-case, and by the Adjutant, who talked a good deal. Shortly afterwards Seargeant-major Goodacre arrived with Captain Gerard and there was a lot of saluting. Spanish hung diffidently to the fringe of the party. The Brigadier said, 'Are we ready?'

Spanish told them, 'Captain Thwaite id'n up yet.'

The Brigadier stared at him and then at the Commanding Officer. 'Who is this?' he said. The Adjutant said it was the Harbour Commissioner.

'Captain Thwaite's in bed,' said Spanish again.

'Oh! Does that matter? Is that important? Who is Captain Thwaite?'

'Captain of the ship, sir,' the Adjutant said.

'What ship?'

'The blockship, sir.' The Adjutant was patient.

'Of course, of course. Well,' he surveyed the party, 'are we all ready?'

They walked along the quayside in the pale sunlight, and as they passed the guard-hut Sergeant-major Goodacre, who was in the rear, made a covert signal to Corporal Foster, who was standing in the wire compound saluting over the wire. 'Sst,' he said and ordered the Corporal to fall in behind and follow him. A little farther on they passed the sentry, who was presenting arms, and Corporal Foster whispered to him, ''Ang about, see?'

Tomlinson fell in behind Corporal Foster.

The Brigadier was saying, 'Remember Gerald Haydon, Henry? Quite a friend of yours, wasn't he?'

'I do, sir,' the Commanding Officer replied. 'I remember him very well. Staff College, Quetta. And Palestine.'

'That's right. I ran into him the other day. He's got a brigade somewhere in the Midlands.'

'Has he? Did very well in Norway, I believe.'

'Extraordinarily good show. Put on a lot of weight recently.'

The Adjutant was saying to the Brigade Major, 'You were all wrong about last week's ammunition return, you know. Looked it up this morning, matter of fact. It's in the third column. There's a balls.'

'Nonsense, old boy. You look again.'

'If you remember, the circular from division said the

practice stuff was to be kept separate from the operational.'

'Oh, division are always wrong. Old Herbert doesn't know his arse from his elbow.'

'Well.'

Behind them Captain Gerard walked alone and in silence. Behind him there was the Seargeant-major and then Corporal Foster and then Tomlinson.

When they reached the ship the Brigadier stopped; was this it? he said, and the Adjutant said it was. They all looked up at the ship.

'Well now,' the Brigadier said, 'what's the problem?'

'Seems to be chiefly a question of rubble,' the Commanding Officer replied. And the Adjutant said at the same time, 'The Captain, sir.'

The Commanding Officer looked at his Adjutant. 'I beg pardon,' the Adjutant said.

'No, you go ahead, Billy; you know more about it than I do.'

The Adjutant explained. Captain Thwaite, he said, was unco-operative to a degree. They had attempted to fill the holds with rubble so that the ship might fulfil her rôle, as blockship, adequately, and all they had from the old man was interference. He had used bad language in front of the men and had thrown equipment into the sea. It was suggested, the Adjutant continued, that the ship be manned by a platoon and made into a strong-point, a sort of floating fortress; a hedgehog, he explained; that the platoon manning the ship should be billeted aboard, where every facility was available for their accommodation; and that the platoon should carry out all the work necessary, such as filling the holds, and defend the ship in case of invasion.

'Sounds quite a good idea,' the Brigadier said. 'What d'you think, Henry?' he asked the Colonel.

'The naval people are very much in favour of it, sir,' said the Adjutant. 'Actually they seem glad to have the thing taken off their hands.'

As he saw it, the Brigadier said, it was entirely a question of fire power. 'How d'you feel about it, Henry?'

The Adjutant said, 'What about those spare Vickers you have at brigade, sir? They'd be awfully useful.'

'Damned if you do,' said the Brigade Major pleasantly. 'They're brand new.'

'What's your reaction, Henry?'

The Commanding Officer hesitated. 'Well, if I may speak frankly,' he said at length, 'I think the whole idea's so much damned nonsense.'

'Oh, do you? That's rather sweeping, isn't it? What's your objection?'

'We're soldiers to begin with, not sailors.'

'Well, we've got to get used to the idea of being amphibious, you know, Henry.'

'Then there's the Captain.'

'Who?'

'Captain Thwaite.'

'He id'n up yet,' Spanish said. He watched the gulls wheeling and crying over the ship and over the heads of the officers.

'He's an infernal nuisance,' the Adjutant said.

'Why isn't he here?' the Brigadier asked. 'Wasn't he warned?'

'Yes, sir,' the Adjutant said. There was a short silence. Spanish sniffed continually and spat into the harbour.

'Send for him, Billy,' the Commanding Officer said. The Adjutant called for Gerard and Captain Gerard summoned the Sergeant-major and Sergeant-major Goodacre nodded to Corporal Foster and the Corporal turned and beckoned Private Tomlinson. 'Get the old man,' he hissed, 'and bloody 'urry.' Tomlinson went off at a lumbering trot down the quayside.

They waited. 'Would you care to go aboard, sir?' the Adjutant suggested at length.

'I don't see why not,' the Brigadier said.

They went up the gangway and stood on the slowly moving deck. Below, the Engineer sang. 'What's that?' the Brigadier demanded. That was the Engineer, Edwards, the Adjutant said. Edwards was on strike in the engine-room. 'Bolshie, sir.'

'Naturalised?'

The Adjutant, not being certain of the Brigadier's understanding, did not answer. They walked up into the bows of the ship past the open hatch, picking their way through the mud and débris that littered the deck. The Brigadier gazed at the sea.

'Splendid field of fire,' he said. 'Wonderful, absolutely wonderful. I see a machine-gun'— he pointed at a spot on the deck — 'here. Possibly two.' He put himself in the position of the machine-guns.

The Commanding Officer made no comment.

'Another,' said the Brigadier, moving over to the port side, 'here. Possibly two here also.'

'What about the bridge, sir?' the Adjutant suggested.

'The bridge? We'll have a look.'

They went up on to the bridge, only Captain Gerard and his Sergeant-major and Corporal Foster remaining on the deck.

'Yes, I think so,' the Brigadier said. 'I don't see why not.' He considered the field of fire. 'I wish that fellow would stop singing.' They fell silent, listening. The bottles rolled to and fro in the wheelhouse. The voice rose and cracked and they heard the violent coughing that followed.

They waited a long time for Captain Thwaite. When at last they saw him on the quayside, the Adjutant leaned over the rail and called down to him, 'Hurry up, man.' The sailor looked up at them. Then he came up the gangway and the ladder to the bridge.

The Adjutant said severely, 'The Brigadier's been waiting,' but the old man made no sign that he had heard. He looked from one to the other, his hands deep in his pockets, his eyes watering in the crisp morning air, without either defiance or humility in his manner.

'They've come, Daniel,' said Spanish in the silence.

'Captain Thwaite,' the Brigadier said, 'I'm happy to meet you.' He was very civil.

'What is it you want?' The old man spoke scarcely above a whisper and the Brigadier did not hear him.

'I said, what is it you want?' He raised his voice.

'Civility, first of all, Captain, common civility.' He was somewhat nettled.

'State your business.'

The Brigadier's eyes narrowed a little. 'I understand you're not co-operating very well with us in the matter of the defence of the harbour.'

'I mind my own affairs.'

'Captain, I'm quite patient. Really most patient.'

'I'm not. What d'you want?'

The Brigadier took a deep breath. 'What are your objections to having a few soldiers on your ship?'

'None,' the old man said.

'What?'

'No objections.' His eyes did not leave the officer's face and watered profusely. Gulls cried over the bridge. 'As many as you like. Plenty of room.'

'I was told otherwise.'

'They're liars, whoever told you.'

'You're changing your tune, Captain Thwaite,' the Adjutant said. 'You told us you were opposed to it.'

The Brigadier shrugged his shoulders. 'I leave it to you, then, Henry. That seems to solve our problem. The sooner you take over the better, I think.'

He bade the sailor good-day.

They left the ship. The old man remained on the bridge and watched them go down the ladder and on to the quayside, where the Commanding Officer issued his orders for the marching in. Gerard's reserve platoon had better do it, he said, and the Adjutant and the Company Commander would remain on board and attend to the accommodation. Then he left them and rejoined the Brigadier, who was walking along the quayside with the Brigade Major. Spanish went on into his office.

"The C.O. seems a little fed-up,' Captain Gerard said. 'Yes,' said the Adjutant briefly.

They would mount the Lewis gun first, the Adjutant said, prefarably in the bows. Sergeant-major Goodacre and Corporal Foster and Tomlinson dismantled the old gun and carried it up the gangway to the deck, the officers following, and mounted it on its tripod on the bows among the lobster-pots and rope and gravel and laid the webbing ammunition buckets beside it on the deck. They put a magazine on the gun. When it was finished, the Adjutant raised the butt to his shoulder and glanced along the sights. It was a magnificent shoot, he said, truly a dream of a shoot. They all tried it. And all the time the old man watched them from the bridge, saying nothing, nor moving, resting his elbows on the rail. Behind him the smoke swirled about the lean funnel and the soldiers caught its bitter stench.

By midday they had finished and they left the ship. The Adjutant would be there, he said, at three o'clock, to supervise the occupation. From the bridge the old man watched them go. When they were out of sight, he went below to the engine-room.

★

TONIGHT, they said in the town, it would freeze again, and moved a little closer to the small bright fires. The low clouds stretched and broke across the sky and their shadows against the sun swept over the sodden earth. The midday train came into the station on the hill, and those who had alighted, and they were few, waited on the platform for the train to leave again, so that Peter Williams might open the gates at the crossing and let them into the town. Yes, it would certainly freeze. They would have another cup of tea, they said, to keep out the cold, and rested their feet on the warm fenders and listened to the news and the tenuous music and felt sleep rising from their bellies and the strange unease of the mines tugging gently at their cables under the surface of the harbour; this they always felt when the town was quiet, as indeed it always was at midday, and stirred, not knowing what it was that lay awake across their minds, till they remembered (and were grateful in a way for the mines in the harbour: in the way they were grateful for the bombers that came in with bombs in the night to drop, but not on Imbleness, and for the Lewis gun that sometimes sent its bullets skipping lazily over the sea towards the enemy, whose only reply was a threat, a shapeless, indefinable bulk like that of death, and bombers that ignored them). And when the boy shouted in the bright street that afternoon they opened their eyes, and when he shouted again and was answered, they woke. There was a lot of shouting suddenly. It was of a different kind, having a different note, from the empty clamour the children generally made playing in the street. A window was thrown up. A door opened. A child ran up the hill crying, with its wooden shoes tapping on the stones. The sagging gate of the house beyond the house adjoining juddered dryly on its hinge and voices rose. They sat up and looked at one another and said What is it?, and rose to go to the window and look into the empty street. The alarm had no form and no character, and so it spread. They went out on to the sidewalk. They waited. And then quite clearly, down the hill near the harbour, a woman screamed. The high sweet sound was lonely in the silence that followed it and moved about the streets alone. There were people running at the foot of the hill. A single figure detached itself from the confusion there and climbed the hill, running. When she came up to those who waited, they ran with her a little way asking What is it? what is it?, and the old woman whose hair drifted over her face had no breath with which to reply. Others followed her, in twos, in families, in groups without number, running up the hill, shouting with panic in their eyes and open mouths towards the level crossing and the reservoir and the rim of the hill. And those waiting did not know whether to go towards the thing they fled from, drawn against their will, or to stay, or to run with those who ran. The ship, they said. The alarm flooded the town. It was the ship. They looked down to the harbour. You could not see whether it moved towards the open sea, or whether it was at anchor, or whether it drifted with the tide towards the mines. Now it was in the middle of the harbour.

They returned during the afternoon, after the foreman of the reservoir, who played dominoes at The Navigator, had climbed the steel ladder that ran up the side of the tower to study the harbour with a pair of binoculars and shouted to those waiting below with upturned faces that the ship was at anchor. They returned slowly, some a little shamefacedly, some angry, and some angry only to cover their shame and outface the derisive smiles of those who had not fled. Already there was a small crowd on the quayside. It grew. And it was an angry crowd, for each man looked a fool in his own eyes at least. They stood in small groups and stared at the ship riding ponderously at anchor in the swell, anchored fore and tied aft to the buoy, and gave voice to their opinions loudly, so that conviction was added and more than those in their immediate vicinity might hear and be drawn into the circle, and of these Uncle O'Hara was especially emphatic. Parliament, he said, should be told. The matter should be looked into. Such a shenanigan. No man, he held, had any right to plant his ship, hitherto tied decently to the jetty, in the middle of the harbour, disturbing the peace, as if the war were not enough, without so much as a kiss your bottom. Spanish, whose traditional reticence stood him now in good stead, shrugged his shoulders and answered none of the questions he as Harbour Commissioner by the grace of God was asked. Before midday, he said, the ship had been where it had been for a year; after midday, it was in the middle of the harbour. He had not been consulted, nor did he know where Captain Thwaite was. He knew nothing. On the ship there was no movement. Smoke dribbled from the stack and was carried down on to the surface of the water by the wind and a dog piddled absently against the capstan round which the ropes, cast from the ship, still lay. The guard knew as little, for Corporal Foster, whose sense of impending trouble was acute, had already addressed his men on the virtue of ignorance. He was nevertheless a little anxious, for the Lewis gun was on the ship, in the bows.

At ten minutes before three a camouflaged truck pulled up outside the Harbour Commissioner's office. It was loaded with kitbags and blankets, with a bicycle, an accordion, a dog, two or three small mattresses, and a gas-stove. The driver lit a cigarette and sat in the cabin of the truck watching the crowd. A few minutes later Lieutenant Allen marched through the gates at the head of his platoon. He was a very young officer and was proud of his men; indeed they marched well, as one man, solidly, irresistibly, indomitably, swinging their arms and setting down their iron heels with conviction, and their equipment shone finely. Lieutenant Allen was looking forward to his new duties, of which he had been told only two hours previously, and thought it was going to be most frightfully amusing. Sergeant Barnaby, who was the tallest man in the platoon and had to shorten his stride considerably to keep the step, did not share Lieutenant Allen's enthusiasm. He was subject to sea-sickness and had the old soldier's distrust of anything new. They marched towards the crowd. The young officer was disturbed to see the ship some little distance from the quayside and wondered whether the Company Commander had made provision for the passage to the ship, down whose side, he now noticed, the gangway hung drunkenly to the water. He was sure it should not have been hanging there like that. The crowd, understanding nothing, opened reluctantly to let them through and then Lieutenant Allen gave the order to halt. They stood at ease a few feet from the edge, facing the ship.

At the officer's request, Sergeant Barnaby fetched Corporal Foster from the guard-hut.

'Why's the ship in the middle of the harbour?'

'Couldn't say, sir,' the Corporal briskly replied. The crowd came closer.

'You mean you don't know?'

'No, sir.'

'When did it anchor there?'

'Couldn't say, sir.'

'What about the sentry?'

'Was looking the other way, sir.'

'Was he?'

'Yes, sir.'

'You're telling lies, Corporal.'

The soldier did not reply. Lieutenant Allen dismissed him and he saluted and returned to the guard-hut and organised well-dispersed fatigues for the remainder of the guard. A few minutes after three o'clock the Adjutant and Captain Gerard arrived at the Harbour Commissioner's office. They walked down the track by the rails towards the platoon. Lieutenant Allen saluted.

The Adjutant demanded immediately, 'Who moved the ship?'

'I don't know, sir.'

A man in the crowd laughed suddenly and was abruptly silenced by his neighbour. The Adjutant moved the glasses a little higher on his nose.

'It was there when I arrived, sir, a few minutes ago,' Lieutenant Allen said.

'What have you done about it, then? Anything? What action have you taken?'

Allen's glance wavered and his eyes dwelled for a moment on Captain Gerard's face. 'None, sir.'

'It's not his fault,' the Company Commander said.

'Send for Corporal Foster.' While he waited, the adjutant looked defiantly round the circle of faces behind him. Their eyes avoided his. They waited patiently. Uncle O'Hara stood with arms akimbo.

Corporal Foster saluted. 'Wish to see me, sir?'

'The ship, man, the ship. How did it get into the middle of the harbour?'

'Don't know, sir.'

'Rubbish, Corporal.'

'I was eating my dinner, sir. Sentry was on the end of the jetty yonder. When I came out, there it was, sir.' He kept his steady gaze on the hairs that grew like a tuft of marsh grass between the Adjutant's eyes.

'Impossible.'

Corporal Foster did not speak.

'Where's Captain Thwaite?'

'Don't know, sir.'

'God damn it, man, you're responsible. You must know something about it.'

Corporal Foster waited, swaying slightly with the wind.
'Well, what do you know about it?'

'Don't know anything, sir.'

Uncle O'Hara interrupted. 'Be God, boy, tell a lie if the truth is awkard.'

'Do nothing of the sort,' the Adjutant said. He swung round and faced the publican. 'You keep out of this,' he told him.

'That I won't,' O'Hara said. 'This is a matter for Parliament.'

'Rubbish! Hold your tongue.'

'It's not the lad's fault,' O'Hara said.

The Adjutant snapped, 'Mind your own business.' He turned to the soldier. 'I'll talk to you later, Corporal.'

The bottle struck the edge of the quay and burst. Fragments of glass struck the Adjutant's long coat, but most of it slithered over the smooth concrete among the feet of the soldiers there. The old man on the bridge of the ship uttered a long wail of triumph and leaned out over the rail, shouting wildly and flourishing his fist, and the voice came dancing over the water, echoing from ship to shore and back again and among the trucks and cottages and up into the town and over the edge of the hill. You could not hear the words, only the cacophonous jet of laughter and abuse and derision. The crowd began to understand and its anger melted in its own ironic laughter. The Adjutant's face lost its colour and he stepped to the edge of the quay and cupped his hands round his mouth, but the voice from the ship did not cease and his hands fell to his sides. He swore aloud.

'We're making fools of ourselves,' Captain Gerard warned him.

'Christ!' the Adjutant muttered. 'This is the last straw.'

Then the old man on the bridge flung another bottle and all their eyes watched it flashing against the sky. But this one fell short into the sea, where it floated for a little while and then sank. Captain Thwaite cursed shrilly and rammed his cap more firmly on to his head and prepared to throw another. The crowd on the quay standing about the platoon of soldiers, now laughing hysterically, took to its heels. The platoon stood fast. No man moved. The third bottle hit the concrete maybe three feet from the Adjutant and burst, and the glass flew among the legs of the soldiers and the label fluttered down the quayside in the wind. The men held firm. Their discipline was excellent.

'March the men to the gate,' the Adjutant ordered.

Lieutenant Allen brought his platoon to attention and marched them away. A bottle landed behind Sergeant Barnaby, who was marching in rear, and he lost the step momentarily.

CAPTAIN GERARD accompanied the Adjutant along the jetty, and the crowd, derisive but disappointed, watched them go. Captain Thwaite left the bridge of the ship in the harbour rearing restlessly from the bower anchor, with the incoming tide building a bow-wave at the stern so that she had the appearance of moving forward through the dark water. The people waited. They waited a long time and dispersed with reluctance; Uncle O'Hara was the last to go.

On the jetty the Adjutant told the Company Commander, 'Something's got to be done, and quickly.'

'Much wiser to let the whole thing drop, Billy.'

'It's gone too far. We've got to get aboard somehow. We can't let the old fool get away with this.'

'Leave me out of it then; I want no part in it.'

'I shall need some of your men.'

'You're asking for trouble. There's nothing he can do. He can only come back, you know. Let it die a natural death. If you're thinking of boarding the ship, think again. Apart from anything else, he's armed. He has the Lewis gun.'

'Are you funking it?' the Adjutant asked him coldly.

'You're a bloody fool, Billy. If you weren't, I'd kick your backside.'

'Don't talk to me like that.'

Gerard interrupted him evenly. 'I don't want any of my men shot trying to redeem your dignity. If the C.O. wants me to do it and it's an order, well and good.'

'He will.'

'How are you going to get there, anyway?'

'I don't know. There are plenty of boats about.'

'And what do you propose to do when you do get aboard? Might as well decide before you get there.'

'We'll see,' the Adjutant said. 'Use force if I have to. Let's go there first.' He leaned over the rail and looked towards the beach. 'One of those cobles might do.'

Rising and falling on the sea, two cobles were heading towards the land. On the beach there were already five, the tracks of the wheels of their cradles running deep in the sand from the white surf to the dry grey sand below the cottages. A few women with shawls over their heads waited at the water's edge. Those who had already beached were selling their catch and you could hear their voices above the stridulation of the gulls. There was a crowd round them, and on the ramp, three trucks and a horse-drawn wagon. The sea beat against the square face of the jetty and the spray drenched the air. The two officers did not hear Watson West behind them. The fisherman waited patiently. At length he coughed and said, 'Excuse me.'

They turned together. He was carrying a parcel under his arm, wrapped in newspaper. He wore long sea-boots up to his thighs and there were fish-scales shining on his jersey and the backs of his red hands.

'Yes, what is it?' the Adjutant asked him.

'I was just wondering ——' He cleared his throat and began again. 'I was just wondering if you'd know of anyone as plays the violin,' he said and hesitated, coughing nervously. 'I thought as you've a lot of men, maybe there's one as does.' He fidgeted with the things wrapped in newspaper under his arm.

'A what? A fiddle?'

'I've asked folks round about, but there's not a one. I thought maybe you'd know of somebody. . . .' His voice trailed away.

'For God's sake, man. No, I don't. And I'm very busy just now.'

'It's just that I've made a one,' Watson West persisted. 'In my spare time I made it.' His eyes flickered from one officer to the other; he unwrapped the instrument and held it out to the Adjutant. 'That's it. It's modelled on a Cremona. An exact model.'

The Adjutant was embarrassed and angry. 'I don't want to see the thing. I know what a fiddle looks like.'

'It's the same as a Cremona,' the fisherman said, 'practically. Cremona was taught how to make them by Stradivarius. A pupil, see? I just wondered if you'd any soldiers as could play it, for to see whether it plays all right. I can't play it myself. My little girl was going to learn, but she got killed in the minefield down yonder. Maybe if you were to ask your soldiers there'd be a one as could try it out. That's all I want to know — if it plays.'

'I can't help you, I'm afraid. Now, please, I'm awfully busy, there's a good fellow.'

Captain Gerard interrupted. 'Yes, I have a man.' He called the sentry from the end of the jetty and, when he came up to them and saluted, told him to find Elwes.

While they waited the fisherman told them, 'I've been at it now for three years in the evenings. Quite a job it's been. I just finished the bow. The bow's not Cremona; it isn't any particular kind. It doesn't matter much about the bow,' he said. 'I just finished.' He drew the bow from the news-paper. A single shining scale clung to the gut and he picked it off carefully. 'That's the bow,' he said.

'May I see the violin?' Captain Gerard asked him.

He unwrapped the parcel again. 'This is it,' he said. His eyes followed it as Allan Gerard turned the instrument over in his hands.

'For Christ's sake!' the Adjutant said and straightening his moustache now flecked with spray and limp, turned away and leaned on the rail.

Watson West's eyes flickered at him expressionlessly and then turned to the instrument in Gerard's hands. 'I'm sorry to be worrying you,' he said. 'I wouldn't if I'd known . . .' he finished lamely.

The sentry went first to the guard-house and afterwards he ran across to the privy whose door was open, and Elwes followed him out with a mop and a bucket in his hands, and Captain Gerard could see them talking together from where he stood. Then Elwes set down the bucket and leaned the mop against the open door and followed the sentry.

He saluted maladroitly and waited.

'You don't salute without a hat in the British Army,' the Adjutant told him briefly, and then, 'Look at yourself. You're a filthy mess, man. Aren't you?'

The soldier's face turned slowly scarlet and he looked at his clothes and the filth on his bare arms.

'Aren't you?'

'Yes, sir. I was on latrine fatigue, sir,' he said, swallowing. Captain Gerard broke in then. 'Elwes, you play the violin, don't you?'

The soldier's eyes drifted away to the horizon. He did not answer.

'Don't you?'

'Yes, sir,' he replied at last.

'It's nothing to be ashamed of.'

Elwes stared at the sea.

Then Captain Gerard turned to Watson West, who undid the parcel again, shielding the instrument from the flying spray with his body.

The fisherman said to Elwes, 'I made it. It's modelled on a Cremona. He was a pupil of Stradivarius.' He held out the instrument to the soldier. 'Play it. Go on, you play it.'

Elwes looked at the Company Commander.

Gerard said, 'He wants you to see what it's like, Elwes. He'd like your opinion.'

Elwes rubbed the palms of his hands slowly against his hips and took the instrument, holding it only with his fingers as though he might crush it. But the hands were confident. He turned it over once or twice and felt the balance. He raised his eyes to Captain Gerard's and then dropped them again to the violin. He flipped the gut. The fisherman watched him closely. The sea pounded at the jettyhead and the swift recoiling waves tilted viciously at those about to break and the wind caught the leaping spray and tossed it at them. Holding it against his belly, Elwes tuned the violin. He put it under his chin and took the bow the fisherman held out to him and picked a fish-scale from the gut; the fisherman said they were all over everything, apologetically. Elwes began to play. He drew the bow twice across the strings. And you saw his nature change. He changed in a subtle way. He had suddenly confidence and assurance and authority. While he played he was alone. He played a few bars at random, and then a scale, and then something which to Gerard seemed familiar. The frail sound fled into the tumult of the sea and the crying of the gulls so that he scarcely heard it.

The fisherman listened and waited.

Elwes held out the violin and the bow to him. 'Good,' he said. 'Wants playing a few years. Salt, sir, won't do it much good.' He turned away up the jetty, but the Adjutant called him back.

'Elwes. You. Come here.'

He returned and waited patiently. In his eyes there was a rare steadiness.

'You stand to attention and then ask to be dismissed,' the Adjutant told him.

'Yes, sir.' He stood to attention.

'And for God's sake try and look a little smarter. You're a bloody disgrace.'

The eyes drifted away to the sea.

'What was it you began to play?' Gerard asked him gently. 'You began to play something.'

'A bit of Brahms, sir.'

'Thank you, Captain Gerard,' the Adjutant said bitterly, and to Elwes, 'All right, dismiss.'

He turned and shuffled away down the jetty.

The fisherman said helplessly, 'It's an exact copy.' He wrapped it in the newspaper. He was dissatisfied and unhappy. 'D'you think he'd play some time for my wife?'

'I should think so,' said Captain Gerard. 'Why don't you ask him?'

'I will. Yes, maybe I will.' He cleared his throat. 'I'm much obliged, much obliged, sir.' He could think of nothing more to say and turned and went after Elwes along the jetty.

Then Allan Gerard said to the Adjutant, 'Was it necessary to speak to the boy like that?'

'Yes.'

The two men faced one another.

'I like my men,' Gerard told him. 'I detest the way you talk to them. Detest it.'

'Currying favour with your own men, that's what you're doing, Gerard.'

'We've just seen something not unlike a miracle, Billy. Did you ever read *Saint Joan*? A miracle is an act which creates faith, or something like that. Well, that was one, the thing we just saw. What it creates faith in, I really don't know. But it creates it all right. It's worth a little trouble. Try and understand.'

'Fiddlesticks.'

'Even so, Billy.'

'We'll win this war, Gerard, and we will, with artillery and infantry and discipline, not fiddles. And just now the discipline in your company leaves a good deal to be desired.'

Gerard looked at him for a moment. His face was white. Then he said, 'Let's forget about it.'

They walked down the jetty leaning back against the wind and saw Hilda Thwaite standing on the edge of the quay, arms akimbo, the heavy blonde hair streaming across her face and into her open mouth as she screamed over the water at her husband, who, neither moving nor replying, watched her dispassionately from the bridge of his ship, leaning his elbows on the rail.

'Come ashore!' she screamed, shaking her fist. 'Come ashore at once or I'll come and get you, you. . . .' Her voice was lost in the wind and she spat the hair angrily from her mouth.

The old man did not move at all.

'D'you hear? Come ashore! You old fool!' She wept helplessly with rage. 'Fool! Fool!' And then, 'I won't be angry with you; I promise I won't say a word. Not a word.' The gulls gathered over her, crying frenziedly. Then she was speaking to herself rapidly. She screamed again, 'Come ashore or I'll fetch the police. . . .'

'Mrs. Thwaite,' the Adjutant began.

She swung on the heel of her slipper and faced him. 'Ah, you! You see what you've done. Perhaps you're satisfied now. A nice mess you've made of everything, haven't you? Haven't you?' she insisted. 'It's all your doing, this. All of it. Look at the old fool now. Well? What are you going to do, eh? It's you who'll bloody do it, whatever it is. You got him out there, now you get him back.'

'My dear woman,' the Adjutant said.

'Wait till I get him, that's all.'

Angry, she was magnificent, thought Captain Gerard. Her big breasts heaved and her eyes glittered like fire.

'Well?' she demanded.

'It's no use blaming me, Mrs. Thwaite,' the Adjutant said. 'Everything possible will be done, rest assured.'

'What, for instance?'

He floundered a little. 'The military authorities will take the necessary action.'

'He won't lose his ship?' she asked him suddenly.

'That's not for me to decide.'

'What, then?'

'I really couldn't say, Mrs. Thwaite.'

They left her and went along the railway-track and heard her begin shouting again behind them, her voice living in the rising wind as though it had come from a great distance. They went into the Harbour Commissioner's office. Spanish did not appear surprised to see them. He was making tea and warming his hands in the steam from the spout of the kettle on the stove. He peered over his shoulder at them.

'I'm just making a cup of tea,' he said.

The Adjutant toyed with his moustache and waited. There was no sound in the little office except the whisper of the kettle and the rattling window.

'You're asking for trouble,' the Adjutant said at length. He cleared his throat. 'Trouble, d'you understand?'

Spanish answered gravely, 'Don't want trouble, sir. No trouble. The last thing I want is any of it. There's trouble enough.'

'You can't run with the hare and hunt with the hounds indefinitely, you know.'

Spanish looked up at him. 'Meaning about the ship yonder? Nowt to do wi' me,' he said briefly, 'any on it.'

'You knew Captain Thwaite was going to move his ship into the middle of the harbour, didn't you?'

'Said nowt to me about it.'

'You knew, nevertheless.'

'Maybe.' He poured the hot water into the teapot carefully and stirred the brew with a pencil.

'How?'

'Some on us knew, mister. We guessed.'

'Rubbish.'

'There were signs. Didn't take much figurin' out.'

'Why didn't you inform me?'

'You didn't ask me.'

The Adjutant felt the spleen rising to his throat. 'That's no reason, man. Answer my question.'

Spanish placed the lid on the pot. 'There's things between sailors as don't need saying. And things between sailors and other folks as can't be said.' He hesitated. 'Cup of tea?'

'No.'

'You, sir?' he asked Allan Gerard.

Gerard shook his head.

Spanish poured himself a cup of tea and blew on the surface of the tea and sipped it, waiting.

The Adjutant drew breath. 'I want a boat,' he said —
'a boat that will hold seven or eight men. With oars.'

'Folly,' said the Harbour Commissioner — 'terrible folly.'

'When I want your valuable opinion,' the Adjutant told
him tartly, 'I'll ask for it.'

Spanish blew on his tea.

'I want the boat tonight.'

'There's mines in the harbour.'

'I know that.'

'It's folly.'

'You won't be held responsible. I'll keep away from the
mines. With room for seven or eight men.'

'Well, you can have a one, if you must.'

'Good. And this time,' the Adjutant added, 'the less said,
the better. Do I make myself clear?'

'It's liable to let a drop of water, the boat,' said Spanish,
blowing and sipping at the tea. 'It needs a bit of caulking.'

'It floats, I take it?'

'Oh, aye, it'll float all right for a while. Wants a bit of
bailing, that's all.'

'Where is it now?' the Adjutant asked him.

'At the foot of the steps.'

'I shall need it at about one o'clock tomorrow morning.
Leave the oars and rowlocks in.'

'I'll see it's ready for you, mister. Will you want any bait?'

'Bait? What for?'

'Fish.'

'I'm not going fishing, man.'

'Ah!' Spanish sipped his tea.

Outside, close to the gates, the platoon waited patiently. Lieutenant Allen paced to and fro in front of them, glancing occasionally at the door of the Harbour Commissioner's office and sometimes, uncertainly, at the ship in the middle of the harbour. He was hurt and angry and felt himself to be ridiculous in the eyes of his men. He felt he had betrayed their trust, and the Company Commander's, in exposing them to the derision of the people of Imbleness. He was very worried about what they thought of him. He did not know, perhaps happily, that, if they thought about him at all, it was with mild pity only. When the Adjutant came out of the office, Lieutenant Allen reported and said,

'May I go aboard, sir? There are some boats by the steps here.'

'No. March your men back to their billets.'

The boy flushed. 'I feel sure I could do something, sir. My men were made to look fools.'

'Do as you're told,' the Adjutant said.

Allen compressed his lips and saluted. The platoon marched out of the gate swinging their arms as they had been taught.

'I shall need a sergeant and six men,' the Adjutant told Gerard, 'at the gate here at half past twelve tonight.'

'Any choice of sergeant?'

'No. Preferably somebody who knows the harbour.'

'Barnaby? That's Allen's sergeant.'

'He'll do.'

'You don't want me, I hope.'

'No.'

'Suppose the C.O. doesn't approve of your trying to board — and I hope to God he doesn't — what then?'

'I'll ring you up in that case.'

'All right.'

But the Adjutant telephoned only to Spanish, to confirm that he would require the boat at the time arranged.

THE Commanding Officer, apart from evincing a certain weariness, raised no objections. To the Adjutant he seemed even more than usually apathetic. He washed his hands of the matter, he said. If that was what the Adjutant wanted to do, and thought could be done, then let it be attempted with all despatch. The Adjutant's enthusiasm was a little dampened by the Commanding Officer's attitude, and he did not understand it, but his resolve only stiffened. He sought in his mind an ulterior motive for the Commanding Officer's easy acquiescence and found none; maybe, he thought, he was being allowed to blunder, and indeed encouraged to do so. Well, there would be no blundering. He was confident. He was convinced he was confident. Damn the C.O. Damn the man. Damn him to hell. His breath clouded the window as he looked out across the dreary leaf-littered garden. He felt alone and in his heart a little afraid. Wet leaves skittered over the grass in the wind.

'By the way, sir,' he said, 'I spoke to Gerard about the discipline in his company this afternoon.'

'What's the matter with it?'

'It's pretty bad, sir. Worst in the battalion.'

'I don't know that I agree, Billy.'

The Adjutant looked into the tired eyes. 'He's too easy with them.'

'Who?'

'Gerard, sir. There's a sort of "happy valley" atmosphere in the company.'

'Can't say I've noticed it. How do you mean?'

'They're still civilians, most of them, and look like it and behave like it. No snap about them.'

'Of course they're civilians.'

'But they've been in the Army damn nearly a year now, sir.'

The Commanding Officer lit a cigarette slowly and with deliberate movements. The Adjutant detested the smile on his face. Then the elder man said,

'I'm very proud of my battalion, Billy. Perhaps extravagantly so. But that's as may be. You didn't see them when they arrived. It was a remarkable sight, I tell you. We were in tents then, that was before you joined the battalion, and it was windy and raining and the camp was a wilderness of mud and half the tents blew away on the first night. But when they arrived, I was standing at the gate watching them come in, still in their civilian clothing, nine hundred and thirty-seven frightened, bewildered, reluctant louts. I was a little depressed, I recall. They were terrifying. I was given eleven officers, all subalterns, and none of them had had any experience at all. I had to make five captains immediately. And I did, to our mutual alarm. But then I saw something happen, Billy, during the few months that followed, which was rather a fine thing to watch. I saw a herd of ragged hoodlums grow into a battalion of infantry. I made a lot of mistakes in handling them, but, thank God, they weren't serious. It seemed to take a long time, but it wasn't very long in fact. We all got tired because it was hard work, but you didn't notice it somehow. My officers made mistakes too, the sort of thing that would seem to us very nearly criminal. They were awful, Billy, those officers, but I wouldn't change them for any in the Army now. I never saw fellows work harder or give more. And the curious thing was that they were working for me, personally. I'm certain they were. You and I do our jobs because we're told to or because we're soldiers always, not just during the war, or maybe because we're ambitious or it doesn't occur to us not to do our jobs, but these civilians cotton on to some particular person for some quite unfathomable reason and do their jobs for him and him only. Good thing to remember, Billy. The ordinary soldiers do things for their company commanders, not for you or me or the Brigadier or the General or the War Office or liberty or democracy or any other bullshit. For their company commanders. Want to remember that. It's rather important, I think.' He played with the cigarette in his fingers and examined it closely. 'My old C.O. in the last war used to say, "You're in the infantry and God help you, and in the infantry all you've got is your own conscience." Something like that.' He frowned heavily.

'About Gerard,' said the Adjutant, shifting to the other foot.

'Oh yes. Yes, Gerard's company. He looked up at the Adjutant. 'Gerard's company's all right,' he said abruptly.

'As you say, sir.'

In a minute the Commanding Officer asked him, 'You're not very happy here, are you, Billy?'

'Yes, sir,' the Adjutant protested, 'only I do hate to see....'

'All right, Billy.'

The Adjutant saluted and left the room.

After he had gone the Commanding Officer lit another cigarette. He sat very still and smoked. He smoked many cigarettes, thinking. He sat smoking for an hour and twenty minutes. There were footsteps outside, but nobody came in. There were no interruptions at all, no distractions, no opportunities or excuses for recoil and postponement.

He used the field telephone when he spoke to the Brigadier and said,

'About my Adjutant, sir. Thought I'd have a word with you.'

The line was bad.

He shouted, 'I wanted to have a word with you about my Adjutant, sir.' Blast the signallers! 'I'm up to establishment, you know, sir. Establishment.'

'Yes, I heard you.'

There was a faint moisture on the Commanding Officer's forehead.

'No chance of promoting him,' he shouted. 'Wondered if you could get him a staff job or something. Camberley.'

'Surprised you want to lose him, Henry.'

'Pity to hold a chap back.'

'Good officer, isn't he?'

The Commanding Officer hesitated. Then he said, Yes, the Adjutant was a good officer.

'What?'

O God! 'Yes,' he shouted, 'he's a good officer.'

'Regular, isn't he?'

'Yes, sir.'

'Hasn't done Camberley, has he?'

'No, sir.'

'Should do, should do.'

'Yes, sir.'

'I'll see what I can do, Henry. Can't promise. Send me a report on him. Better make it a good one.'

'Very well, sir.'

'Might get him a month or two at division. Good training. I'll have a word with the General.'

'Thank you, sir.'

'Can't hear you.'

'I said thank you, sir.'

'Oh! Not a bit. That all?'

'Yes, sir.' He put down the receiver.

In the next war, he supposed, the Adjutant would be commanding a division or a corps or something and would do very well until he was found out, only a great many men would have to lose their lives first. Well, that has nothing to do with me, the Commanding Officer told himself. Maybe there wouldn't be another war. Maybe the Adjutant would have been retired by then. Anything, anything might happen. He listened to the Regimental Sergeant-major mounting the guard. Their boots rang on the cobbles outside. The R.S.M. was a good man. Damn glad to have him in the battalion. Absolutely first class. They were all good men. The Commanding Officer loved his battalion dearly.

In the dusk Spanish rowed out to the ship.

The frost had begun to settle. Darkness did not fall from the sky, but rose from the earth upwards, flowing out of the sea over the land to reach up to the clouds from the summit of the hill behind the town. When the land was quite dark, then the night spread evenly across the sky.

Water swilled about the bottom of the boat. He rowed stiffly, tugging at the frayed oars and glancing over his shoulder from time to time as he drew close to the ship. As he rowed he watched the lights twinkling on the hillside and going out one by one. The boat danced decorously in the swell, nudging the wide rusty flank of the ship, and he fended off with the oar, for, being empty and high out of the water, the ship rolled perilously. He made fast to the gangway that still drooped down the side and, testing it with his weight, climbed slowly up on the deck. Captain Thwaite was on the bridge.

'I was expecting you, Spanish,' he said. He was leaning over the rail.

Spanish stood beside him.

The old man narrowed his eyes at the open sea. 'It's cold,' he said; he said; 'it's cold up here, Spanish.'

'Freezing again.'

'When are they coming?' the old man asked him at length.

'Tonight.'

With each rolling wave the ship rose and then plunged, creaking and straining, alive with sounds. When the wind rested, you could hear the Chief Engineer singing below. The ropes slapped at the mast. The old man looked down at the Lewis gun in the bows and the open hatch and the rubble that littered the deck.

'I thought, maybe, you'd want to get ashore a bit,' said Spanish.

'Yes, that's very kind of you.'

'I thought you'd have one or two things you'd want to be doing.'

'No. I don't think so, particularly. I want to see Mrs. Thwaite, that's all.'

'She's there.'

'Yes, she there all right.'

In a minute the old man asked him, 'Did you ever touch Oran?'

'Where?'

'Oran.'

'No. Casa. Algiers.'

'No. Oran.'

'No, never touched it.'

'Finest woman I ever knew was a whore in Oran, in a brothel. She was a beauty. Portuguese. I always remembered her.'

'Never touched Oran, myself.'

The old man said again, 'She was a beaut.'

Far to the north a searchlight wandered aimlessly across the sky and went out. Then there was another.

'Must have been thirty years ago,' he said. 'Oran was a stinking hole. Always remember the way it stank. Funny the way you remember smells.'

'I never went there.'

'By God, it smelled.'

Spanish changed his position a little. 'Algiers I remember.' He drew breath deeply to clear the reminiscence from his heart. He said, 'Where's the Chief?'

'Below.'

'Maybe he wants to go ashore.'

'No. I asked him; he doesn't.'

They left the ship. Spanish rowed and the old man sat in the stern with his feet in the bilge looking towards the quay vacantly. His eyes were now a little bloodshot with the rare sobriety. He pulled at his empty pipe. The boat was not seen. Indeed, against the black water it was invisible. The rowlocks creaked and Spanish grunted with each brief pull. They moored the boat at the foot of the steps below the Harbour Commissioner's office and went up on to the quayside and, crossing the railway, whose rotting sleepers were already silvered with frost, went into the inn. In the saloon, where there was a fire and a yellow shaded light above the dartboard on the wall, Uncle O'Hara was leaning through the hatch in the wall talking to somebody in the parlour you could not see; the braces hung from his waist almost to the ground. He withdrew carefully when he heard them calling, and when he saw who it was his mouth fell open.

'Glory be to God,' he said.

'Good evening, O'Hara. Two large tots of rum.'

The publican set his arms akimbo. 'Y'ould pirate, you,' he said, his voice rising.

'The rum, please.'

'Man, it's delighted I am to see you. Never in all me born days,' he said, 'did I see more hell raised in a place than I saw with me own eyes this afternoon, Captain Thwaite. Magnificent, it was — magnificent! There's not a boy in the town as knows whether it's a shit, shave, or a shampoo he's wantin'. I raise me hat, sir, in gratitude and admiration, though, mind, you, it's a terrible pity, and a great and grievous pity you're not a better shot with the bottle. Not that I'm complainin' — far be it from me. Be God, it was a sight as did me ould heart good. The whole bloody place is in a ferment, Captain. Did you know? Half the town trapesin' up the hill yonder, frightened out of their wits you'd drift on to the mines, and the other half gapin' on the quayside, and me among them. I saw it, every darlin' moment. I was there. Praise be to God, I was there. The first thing that's happened in this lousy town I haven't missed. Jesus, Mary, and Joseph! Two rums.' He set the glasses on the bar. 'Have this, me boys, on the house.'

They drank.

'But it's trouble you're askin' for, showin' your nose at all just yet. Confidentially' — he lowered his voice and leaned over the bar — 'confidentially, there's one or two boys on the lookout for you, Captain Thwaite. And I'm not surprised, be God. Take the military, for instance. That Adjutant fellow's lackin' in sense of humour. It seems the dignity of the military is at stake. And there's a certain lady, no names, no pack drill, who is swearin' fit to murder. In your shoes, Captain, I'd be lettin' things die down a bit and get from under.'

'Two more rums, O'Hara.'

'Have you money to pay? For she won't, not after this afternoon.'

Spanish said, 'I'll be paying.'

'What is it you're back for, anyway?'

'Is Mrs. Thwaite at home?'

'She is.'

LYING on her bed she cried, 'Who's there?' when the old man tapped on the door, and when she heard his voice she got up and opened it, not believing that it was indeed her husband. She stared at him, astonished, as he stepped into the room saying, 'Hello, Hilda,' shyly, with a little smile, and his hands in the pockets of his coat. The soles of his rubber boots whispered faintly on the smooth linoleum.

She closed the door.

'Well,' she said flatly. She examined his face and saw with a slight misgiving that he was sober. His eyes were bloodshot and he narrowed them against the light and a muscle in the left side of his face twitched. But he was sober. And there was something in his manner she could not identify at once, a kind of personal satisfaction that lent him an air of detachment. He was hugging something to himself, she felt, pleased with it, and it had nothing whatever to do with her. She did not understand the way he looked at her.

'Well,' she said again, uncertainly now.

'Well, Hilda.'

'So you've come back.' Her voice was husky, for her throat was sore and painful.

'It looks like it.' He sat on the edge of the bed and smiled at her.

'Pleased with yourself, aren't you?'

'Medium.'

She waited.

'You should have seen it, Hilda.' He laughed softly to himself. 'You ought to have seen it.'

'Old fool.' Her voice rose and she coughed. 'What have you come back for?'

He shrugged his shoulders. 'I've come back home. Where else am I supposed to go?'

She demanded suddenly, 'What's at the back of your mind?'

'Nothing, Hilda.'

'Don't think you're fooling anybody. You're not.'

'My dear, I wouldn't dream of it. I've come back, that's all. Begin talking.'

She whispered, 'Talking?'

'Aren't you going to be angry with me?' he asked her. 'I expected you'd be very angry indeed. You wanted to see me, didn't you?'

'Yes.'

'Well, begin.'

She could not think of anything adequate to say that would reach him. He seemed to be laughing at her and, in an odd friendly way, asking her to share the joke. She felt maladroit and inarticulate.

'Aren't you going to say anything?'

'Plenty.'

'Well, go on, then.'

She was silent, fumbling for words.

He said simply, 'But I've ruined everything, haven't I? Everything's absolutely ruined, isn't it, because of what I did this afternoon? I did speak to the military authorities, you know — I promised I would, didn't I? — and told them to go ahead and put the soldiers on the ship. I said to the Brigadier, "I've no objection." But then I moved the ship into the middle of the harbour. Seems to have caused a bit of a to-do by all accounts, with people running up the hill and one thing or another, thinking I'd drift into the minefield. Then when they did turn up, all marching along the quayside there, I threw bottles at them, damn near hit them too, and they went off in a huff, and then you came along and began shouting, only I couldn't hear you because of the wind. It's no good shouting into the wind, my dear. I heard you, though; I heard you all right, but I didn't take any notice. That was deliberate, Hilda. I deliberately pretended not to hear, and I'm sorry if you hurt your throat shouting — it sounds a bit sore. I only wanted to make you angry. You shouldn't have gone on so long.'

He watched her expectantly. Quite soon she would have to say something, she knew, something pungent, or even purely violent, to prevent herself sitting down in the chair by the bed and laughing in a high, flat voice. She was bewildered and somewhat afraid. She struggled for anger, but it would not come. It was a stranger who knew her too well who talked to her, calmly sitting on her bed. But it is my husband, she told herself, this is Daniel. She gazed at him, striving to read his mind. No, she could not tell. His eyes were pleased and interested and she could not tell whether his terrible innocence was assumed or genuine. It occurred to her suddenly that he might be mad.

'I shouldn't think the owners will stomach it,' he said amiably, 'not when they know. And the naval authorities will certainly tell them. Maybe the pension will be stopped after all. I hope it's not. I'm sorry, Hilda. I do hope that doesn't happen, for your sake. You deserve it after all this time.' He took out his pipe and sucked at it reflectively. 'It's been a longish time.' He examined the bowl of his pipe and then put it back in his pocket. 'I'm very sorry it happened. It just happened, that's all.' He smiled to himself. 'I had the time of my life.' He laughed silently, his loose bulk shaking. 'Unbelievable. I just don't credit it, d'you know? You shouldn't have tried to interfere, though, Hilda. Great mistake. Standing there shouting for the police. You ought not to have done that. And you did look so damned pathetic trailing home along the quayside when you'd given up trying. I felt sorry for you.'

'Stop it,' she said abruptly, 'stop it, stop it.'

'What's the matter?'

She was trembling. 'Don't imagine you're fooling any-body, Captain Thwaite.'

'No, I don't,' he said soberly. 'Why don't you get angry? Then you'll feel better.'

'Angry! Dear God!'

'That's better.'

'What's the matter with you?' she persisted. 'There's something the matter with you.'

'No.' He smiled at her. 'No, I haven't gone crazy.'

'You're acting like it.'

'Am I?'

'What are you trying to hide?'

'Nothing. I've nothing to hide. I'm an old man; there is no reason for me to hide anything now.'

'There's something in the back of your mind,' she per-sisted.

He hesitated and then said evenly, 'Are you leaving me?'

She turned away. 'I haven't decided,' she said.

'You're not.' He spoke as though to himself.

'I said I hadn't decided, didn't I?' Her voice rose and rasped in her throat.

'Nevertheless, you're not.'

'Don't drive me to it, Daniel,' she warned him.

He said No, gravely, no, he would not drive her to it.

Then she began to speak. 'No,' she said, 'I'm not going to leave you. That would be fine if I did, wouldn't it? Just what you'd like, for me to clear out and leave you to go your own sweet way.' She felt somewhat better. 'Well, there's nothing doing. I'm not going, now or any other time, see? No matter what happens, for better or for worse, in sickness or in health, I'll be right here by your side, dearie.' She felt splendid now, suddenly, and stronger. 'And don't imagine it's all over and forgotten about, what you've done to me this afternoon, chucking away all I've slaved for and longed for all these years, a chance of a bit of peace and quiet and a bit of freedom — don't imagine just because I haven't said anything it's all over and done with. You'll pay for the crime you've done to me on your deathbed, Mister Captain bloody Thwaite. Every day and minute of your life you'll pay. You'll regret it. You'll wish you'd never been born. You'll rue the day. Because I'm staying, see? I'm not leaving you. I'm your wife. And from now on you're going to do as I want. Me. D'you hear?' Her voice rose again. 'And I'm going to do as I want, just exactly what I want, never mind whether you like it or not. Damn you! Damn what you think! It's what I think that's going to matter. You've had your say, you had it this afternoon, you had enough say for a lifetime this afternoon, and some to spare. Sorry, are you? Sorry! You're going to be sorrier than you ever dreamed about. You'll come to me on your bended knees before I've done with you. You'll beg me to let you go. Sorry! God!' She flung back the hair which had fallen across her face. 'And just to start right, just to give you the general idea, you didn't know about me and O'Hara, did you?' She could not stop now. 'You didn't know what's been going on under your nose, did you, eh? That O'Hara's been seeing me practically every afternoon while you've been sleeping off your drink? You didn't know about that, did you?'

He lowered his eyes, rubbing the stubble on his chin meditatively. 'Yes, Hilda,' he said quietly, 'I've known for a long time.'

'Well, that's how it's going. . . .' Her voice trailed away and her mouth fell open.

'I've known since it began.'

She did not speak.

'Did you think I didn't?'

She said in a high voice, 'You never said. . . .'

'No, I didn't say anything.'

She began to laugh hysterically, standing in the middle of the room with the light shining on her blonde hair.

He watched her. 'Stop laughing,' he said at length.

He felt the blood rising to his head and he swallowed and constricted the muscles of his throat to keep it back.

'Please stop laughing.'

She opened her eyes momentarily in surprise and stared

at him, and then went on laughing, arms akimbo and legs wide.

'Hilda.'

She did not seem to hear him.

'Hilda.'

He stood up, knowing suddenly that he could no longer control it, that it was too old and strong for him and too white-heated, and struck her wildly, a great swinging blow with the back of his hand across her mouth. Her mouth was open and so the sound had a curious hollow ring that drifted about the room in the silence that followed it. He could not stop now. 'Bitch,' he whispered, 'bitch, bitch, bitch, bitch,' striking her to and fro across the face each time as she fell back, till he had no more breath. She hit the wall and lost her footing on the smooth linoleum and slipped down the wall slowly.

For a moment he listened to his own hoarse breathing. He straightened his coat with bleeding fingers and opened the door. He turned and loooked at her. There was an expression of overwhelming surprise on her face and a trickle of blood ran down her chin from her lips. She made no sound. He closed the door again and went to her and bent over her, touching her with a fluttering hand, saying, 'Better get up, Hilda.' He took her arm. 'Come along.' He put his arm round her waist and helped her to the bed. She swayed against the dressing-table and the mirror swung loose on its hinge. 'There, there,' he whispered. 'Lie down. Thatsaway.' She lay under the pretty rainbow that the bevel of the mirror cast over the bed and over her legs. He held the

towel under the tap for a moment and wrung it out carefully and carried it across to her. Taking her head in his
arm he bathed her lips. He bathed her eyes. 'Thatsaway,' he
kept saying, 'that's a good girl.' The cheap scent clung to
the hair that lay across his shoulder. He pushed it away
from her face, but it fell back again. 'Upsadaisy,' he said,
and pushed it back. When he had finished he let her head
fall back gently to the pillow and hung the towel over the
back of the chair close to her hand. He then left the room.

SPANISH was still there, in the saloon, when he returned.
'Hello,' he said affably. He was very happy, for there was a
calm in his heart now, a full sweet peace such as he had not
known for years. He was in sympathy with everything in
the orbit of his mind's eye. Towards the Harbour Commissioner he felt friendly and benevolent, and they stood side
by side at the bar feeling the friendship without a word
spoken.

'Rum?' said the Harbour Commissioner.

'Yes.'

Uncle O'Hara said, 'Who's to be payin' for this?'

'I am,' Spanish replied.

'You'll get drunk,' Spanish warned the old man.

After a time they had another drink.

'Perish the thought,' said Captain Thwaite happily.

Furtively now Uncle O'Hara watched them. Something had happened and he was worried that he knew nothing of it. He was vexed. Here was something else going on in his own establishment of which he was completely ignorant.

'That was a most impressive manoeuvre of yours this afternoon, Captain, if I may say so,' Spanish said. 'In the harbour.'

'Two lengths of good rope I slipped.' Nevertheless he was much gratified.

'I fancy the authorities won't let you stay there very long, however.'

The old man said, 'I didn't like losing that rope. Best manilla, it was.'

'They'll be after you.'

'Let 'em.'

'They're too strong for you. Too strong for any man by himself.'

Captain Thwaite leaned across the bar. 'Do you find the conversation interesting, Uncle O'Hara?'

'I wasn't listenin',' said the publican, looking up.

'Just your ear was twitching a bit.'

'I wasn't listenin',' said O'Hara stubbornly.

Captain Thwaite thrust out his underlip. 'Bloody hyena,' he said as though to himself. Then he laughed a little, his great stomach shaking. 'Poor old O'Hara,' he said.

'What's the matter now?'

'It's beautiful to think on. Just looking at you and thinking what's coming does me good.' They would have another drink, he said.

There was nobody else in the saloon and it was so quiet you could hear the flames of the fire; every sound was clear and identifiable. Uncle O'Hara squeezed his shoulders through the hatch and talked loudly to the men playing dominoes in the parlour, to escape the misery of ignorance in the saloon. Captain Thwaite's eyes glazed as the liquor rose to his head. But now it did not stupefy and glove his wits. It polished them. Now he felt fine and powerful and dynamic and there was nothing he was not capable of doing. He began to hum in his throat. Soon he would stroll down to the quay and down the steps outside the Harbour Commissioner's office to the boats and scull slowly out to the ship. There was plenty of time.

Then it was late, quite suddenly it was late, and he was alone. He had been sitting in the parlour too long. He pulled himself up out of the chair and straightened his cap and put his pipe away in his pocket and went out. The utter depths of the night were the more impenetrable because he had sat too long in front of the fire watching the flames dancing in the bright brass shovel in the hearth, and the bitter wind lent fresh virulence to the liquor in his stomach, and he halted blindly, stretching out a hand to the wall. Gaudy screens bestrode his narrowed eyes. He began to walk in the direction of the steps. Then dimly he could see the rail against the frosted earth and the edge of the quay and the towering bulk of the waggons. The sea sucked in the weeds at the foot of the steps. A long way away, on a level with his head, there was a light: in the guard-house beyond the buffers. Then there was somebody walking along the quayside towards him. He could not hide. He waited. It was Allan Gerard.

The soldier stopped. 'Who's that?' he asked.

'Me. Captain Thwaite.'

'Oh, it's you, Dan.' He came closer. 'Where are you off to?' The question was casual and easy, a politeness; but the answer was difficult.

'Oran,' he said.

'Where?'

'Oran.'

Gerard laughed. 'Daniel, you're drunk again.'

'Maybe.' He waited for the soldier to go. He could not tell what Gerard was thinking; it did not matter, only that he should go quickly. When he spoke again, the soldier's voice had changed.

'I hope the weather keeps fine for you,' he said. He turned and went away into the darkness. Daniel Thwaite drew a deep breath.

He went down the steps to the sea and fumbled in the wall for the ring to which the rope was tied that moored the boat. In the boat the bilge-water was cold over his feet. He cast off and the little boat pitched wildly in the swell and on the wind he caught the pungent stench of smoke. When he came close to the rolling mass of the ship, seeing nothing in the darkness but sensing her proximity, he felt the sea calmer under her lee and heard the Engineer's voice, but only when the Engineer essayed the higher notes as though the voice came from the sky and the bed of the sea and with the wind from its very source. He climbed up the swaying gangway and shoved at the boat with his foot, thinking what a pity it was, the boat needed only a little attention. Maybe Spanish would recover it, on the beaches to the south, in a day or two.

He went below and forward to the cable locker, feeling his way along the familiar passages, down the iron ladders into the hull. The whole ship creaked and strained and muttered as she rose and plunged, and below the din was magnified many times. Rats scattered squealing from beneath his feet, and when he struck a match their eyes shone momentraily in the flame. He wrenched at the door of the cable locker and in a minute it came open. Inside he lit another match and, holding it aloft, clambered over the sleeping cable to the clench and dragged the chains aside till he could get at the shackle and kick the pin out; it was stiff in the rust. Above his head the chain hanging from the navelpipe swung with the motion of the ship, sometimes striking the plates, up through the choked pipe to the deck and running supine along the boards to the windlass where it was held fast; the windlass took the weight of the anchor. From the windlass to the hawsepipe it would be stiff and taut and grinding quietly against the worn steel. He hated slipping the anchor, but the donkey-engine was cold and the cylinder was cracked anyway, and so there was no way of taking in the anchor; you could only slip it. He looked again at the shackle. In the matchlight the walls of the locker ran with water and the chain swung and the ship strained and ponderously worried at the thing holding her to the bed of the harbour. He left and went back on deck and forward to the windlass below the bridge, slipping a little on the frosted boards. Standing close to the machine, he leaned his weight against the brake lever. The hub of the machine turned, quite slowly at first, then at once faster as the vessel soared on a long inrolling wave, shaking herself free. Jerking and now alive the cable moved across the deck, each separate link drumming on the shoulder of the hawsepipe, faster all the time, faster and faster into the sea, till the ship throbbed like a fevered heart and the last fathom whirled and crazily flailed the splintering boards as the windlass spun. Then it was gone. The bows swung round slowly.

He ran to the wheelhouse and signalled dead slow ahead to keep her bow-on to the open sea while he went to the stern to cut the ropes that held her there to the buoy. Edwards started engines and in a little while, quietly, with infinite stealth, the ship slipped out of the harbour.

At that time Elwes was on duty. He did not hear the ship leave the harbour. He was leaning over the rail of the jetty with Winslow, who was on duty with him, their two-hour spells overlapping during an hour. They talked a little in the dark. Sometimes they took a short walk, alone, to the gate and back, perhaps going into the privy to take a pull or two at the cigarettes each had been smoking for an hour and a half. (The wall of the privy was measled with small black burns where the cigarettes had been stubbed.) They could hear the early fishermen moving about the cobles on the beach, because the wind had veered a point or two from the east to the south-east, but they neither saw or heard the *Ur of the Chaldees*. Elwes did not want to talk because he had things to think about. This afternoon he had said to Watson West that he would come and play the fisherman's violin tonight in the cottage above the beach; he would play for them both, but especially for Mrs. West. He had promised to go at about midnight, after the fisherman had slept and before he went out again. It would mean talking to Winslow about it, that was the difficulty, so that Winslow might take the full burden of the duty for half an hour; Winslow, if anything went wrong, might have to lie, and he would have to tell Winslow where he was going and for what reason, and though Winslow was a gentleman, quite a gentleman, a companionable accommodating fellow, nevertheless the notion of speaking of something so near to him and so intimate was alarming and he shied at it. Winslow, too, he expected, would be embarrassed.

He said presently, 'I wonder if you'd do me a bit of a favour, Winslow.'

'What's that?' The soldier spat idly into the sea.

'Well, I was wondering if you'd mind if I pushed off for half an hour.' He blew his nose and coughed. 'I don't like asking you. Just a half-hour or so. I wouldn't be long.'

'What for, change your socks?'

'No, it isn't a girl.' He hesitated.

'What then?'

'I promised to go to a man's house, this afternoon. I promised I'd go, you see, tonight.'

'All right,' said the soldier, 'if you don't want to tell me. It's your bloody funeral, though. I can keep my mouth shut.'

'I wasn't thinking you'd talk. That wasn't it.'

Winslow turned to him in the dark. 'Yes, you were. Don't try and kid me. Suggesting I'd talk.'

'I didn't suggest any such thing, Winslow.'

'Yes, you bloody did. I take a poor view.'

'I know you wouldn't talk. I never dreamed of it.'

'You said,' he drew breath, 'you said. . . .' He turned away impatiently. 'Well, I wouldn't, that's all.'

'Of course not.'

'Christ, if we're all going to start kicking each other up the arse every time we turn our backs after bloody nigh a year, what's the use?'

'I quite agree, Winslow,' said Elwes patiently, and in a moment, 'Would you mind, then, if I went? To tell the truth, it's one of those fishermen, he's made a bit of a violin and I've said I'd play it for him.' He waited. 'Can't play it himself.'

'I don't want to know where you're going,' said Winslow. 'I'm not interested in where you're going at all.'

'I was just telling you.'

'I said I don't want to know, didn't I? Didn't I just say I wasn't interested?'

'Yes.'

'Well, then. Go on. Get moving. I'll be here.'

'All right.' He shouldered his rifle. 'I'm greatly obliged to you.'

'For Christ's sake.'

'I'll be back in half an hour.'

'Anyone would think I was giving you a million fornicating pounds,' Winslow remarked bitterly.

Elwes did not reply.

'Ask them if they've any tobacco,' Winslow said.

'What sort?'

'Any. Donekal Aromatic Plug I practically always smoke, but I don't suppose he's got any of that.'

'I'll ask him.'

He went down to the jetty and passed the guard-house quietly, because he did not want to make it difficult or embarrassing for Corporal Foster, who had enough responsibility as it was, and on to the gate, where he turned to the left into the quiet street and walked along to Watson West's cottage, which was last but one in the row, and tapped on the door.

Watson West opened it and Elwes said, 'I've come,' and stepped into the little room, leaning his rifle in the corner by the door and taking off his helmet shyly. The room smelled of paraffin oil and, faintly, of fish.

Allan Gerard found O'Hara in the saloon. There was nobody else in the room. The fire burned brightly and the glasses on the shelves shone beyond the dome of the Irishman's head. O'Hara looked up from the newspaper he was reading and saw Gerard and nodded. The soldier leaned against the bar and lit a cigarette.

'We might get some snow soon,' he said.

'I'll have a glass of beer, I think.'

O'Hara served him.

While the publican busied himself, Gerard watched him. At length he asked him, 'Uncle O'Hara, did Mrs. Thwaite happen to mention to you a conversation I had with her on the subject of the *Ur of the Chaldees*?'

O'Hara shrugged his shoulders. 'She might have, and she might not. There's a lot goin' on, you know, and I don't remember everything.'

'She had a talk with the Adjutant too, didn't she? And then with her husband.'

'She talks to all manner of people. A charmin' woman.'

'Did you warn her of the possible consequences of her interference in the matter of her husband's ship?'

Uncle O'Hara looked up at him now. 'I think the lady must have called your bluff, Captain Gerard.' He smiled and folded the newspaper and rested his arms on the bar, still smiling, looking at the soldier. 'It must be very difficult for you.'

Gerard nodded. 'It is,' he agreed. 'What do you think we ought to do? Anything?'

'Well, now.' He rubbed the folds of his chin. 'I should think keepin' your nose out of other people's business would be a good start, Captain sir. Then again you might offer a few touchin' apologies to those parties you've been castin' aspersions at, me included. After that, all bein' well, I'd suggest a little service of thanksgivin', with the choir, for your errin' soul's sake, for it's deliverance from a unfortunate position if ever I saw one, the lady havin' taken the matter into her own fair hands, and the hell with both of us, especially you.'

'Yes. There's something in that. Suppose, however, that Captain Thwaite disappeared one night? Suppose, for the sake of example, that he was drowned. What would your position be then, *vis-à-vis* Mrs. Thwaite?'

O'Hara said smoothly, 'The lady would have my profound sympathy in her great bereavement.'

Gerard laughed. 'You're an amusing scoundrel, O'Hara.'

'Me mother always said, and she dead twenty years now, always said I'd be wastin' me time doin' anythin' honest, so I do me poor best to affect a decent compromise.'

They heard the woman's voice then, in the parlour, calling. She was calling her husband's name. Allan Gerard looked at O'Hara. They went into the parlour together and she turned on them. She had been weeping, they saw at once, and there were red weals across her mouth.

'Where's Daniel?' she demanded.

Gerard raised his eyebrows. 'Has he gone?'

'You!' She narrowed her eyes. 'You're responsible for this. Where is he?'

O'Hara interrupted evenly. 'Calm yourself, Mrs. Thwaite. Your husband's safe and sound.' He patted her on the arm and she shook him off angrily. 'What's been happenin' to your beautiful face?' he said.

She touched her mouth. 'That's where my husband beat me.'

Gerard said, 'The brute.'

'Monstrous,' said O'Hara.

'You be careful, Uncle O'Hara,' she warned him. 'It's sympathy I expect from you. Where's Daniel?'

Gerard said he had seen Captain Thwaite a few moments previously on the quayside, and she replied at once, 'It's pitch dark. I've been out.'

'I spoke to him.'

'Where was he going? I've got to see him.'

'Oran.'

'Where?'

'Oran, he said. I didn't quite understand. I asked him where he was going and he said, Oran.'

She touched her broken lips. She watched him steadily for the trace of a smile in his face, but there was none. 'Where's Oran?' she asked in a moment.

'North Africa.'

'Was he drunk?'

Allan Gerard said that Thwaite had seemed sober enough.

'Oran, Oran? What's he playing at?'

And then Gerard said briefly, 'Guess.'

There was a long silence in the room. Somewhere in the building there was water running through a pipe. The windows rattled a little and the fire hissed gently. The woman's face was still and she moved her fingers over her lips. Then her eyes, fixed on the soldier's face, dilated.

O'Hara whispered, 'By God, the minefield.'

She sat down at the table in the middle of the room and her shoulders sagged forward. She began to sway to and fro, rocking herself on the chair and uttering small sounds in her throat with her hands against her face and her knees drawn up. O'Hara went to the window and drew aside the curtain and peered out.

'He's gone,' Gerard said.

O'Hara let fall the curtain and turned, arms akimbo.

'What have I done that he should do this to me?' Hilda Thwaite cried.

'Now, now, Mrs. Thwaite,' the publican said, 'let us not jump to any foolish conclusions. Because the old man's disappeared a minute there's no need to suppose he's a goner. He knows well enough there's a minefield out yonder.'

'He's gone,' she whispered, and louder, 'he's gone.'

'Now listen to reason ——'

'He'll suffer for this,' she said.

'He's havin' a little jest, that's all. He'll be shufflin' in here again in a minute askin' for his rum, you'll see.' But he was uneasy in his heart and you could hear it in his voice.

She swung round to him. 'Why don't you do something to find him, instead of standing there talking?'

'You were the only one who might have done anything, Mrs. Thwaite,' Allan Gerard told her. 'The ship will have left the harbour by now.'

With great joviality Uncle O'Hara said again that Captain Thwaite would return. 'Mark my words. He's givin' us a bit of a fright just for the fun of it ... to teach the military a lesson.'

'The military.' She got to her feet, the colour rising to her face. 'The military. Damn the military! Why can't they leave things alone? Everything was all right before they started interfering. Now look. I'll sue them, that's what I'll do,' she stormed. 'I'll have the law on them; I'll take them to court.' She uttered a sob, and turned her back on the two men; they listened to her heavy breathing. 'I can't stand this, I can't stand it much longer. Why doesn't somebody stop him? He may not have gone yet. He's got to be stopped.'

O'Hara said patiently, 'Don't I keep tellin' you he'll be comin' through that very door in two shakes of a lamb's tail, pleadin' for his drop of rum? Now quiet yourself, Mrs. Thwaite, and don't be disturbin' the rest of us,' for he was very disturbed and there was a moisture on his forehead.

When Spanish entered and stood in the doorway, they fell silent. He looked from one to the other.

'The blockship's gone,' he said.

Hilda Thwaite opened her mouth to scream, but no sound passed her lips.

'She put to sea a minute or two ago.'

Now she said, 'I knew it, I knew it. I told you. Didn't I tell you?' She wrung her hands. 'He's got to be stopped,' she cried. 'He must be stopped. Spanish,' she flung out her arm a thim. 'I demand that you stop that ship.'

Spanish sniffed. ' I doubt there's much me or anyone else can do now, ma'am. And I don't think the old man would let us, even if we could.'

'He's crazy,' the woman cried; 'he doesn't know what he's doing. What have I done for him to leave me like this if he knew what he was doing? He's drunk.' She grasped at the straw. 'Yes, he's drunk. That's it. That's what it is. O'Hara's deliberately made him drunk.'

Spanish ignored her. 'I was on the jetty and she went past me with scarcely a sound,' he murmured. 'I couldn't see her, but you could hear the old engines beating like a girl's heart in the night, and a bottle rolling to and fro on the bridge as she took the swell."

She sat on the arm of the chair and wept tears of rage and mortification.

'That's a terrible thing,' the Irishman muttered.

But Spanish shook his head. 'He's happy enough, I reckon. He's found himself.'

'It's terrible to think of,' O'Hara said —'the minefield.' He added, more cheerfully, that the old man had not far to go, God rest his soul. 'Will we hear it, the explosion?'

Spanish said yes, they would hear it.

'You could stop him if you wanted,' the woman said. 'You're to blame.'

'There's nothing we can do, woman,' Spanish told her testily. 'Let him go in peace.'

'Anyone would think I was to blame the way you talk,' she said. 'Haven't I always been a good wife to him? He's a bad man to do this to me. All my life I've slaved for him and nursed him and worked my fingers to the bone. I've given him more than any man has a right to ask of a woman.'

Allan Gerard, who had been sitting at the desk below the windows, rose and moved towards the woman. She was surprised to see him, having thought him gone or forgotten that he was still in the room. 'You really mean that, don't you, Mrs. Thwaite? It'll be a great help to you in the years to come to know that you were a good wife to him.' She was one of those women, he said, who are capable of convincing themselves of anything, even their own virtue, at a moment's notice. 'And so you never suffer.'

'Nobody can deny I was a good wife to him,' she retorted. 'Nobody. Better women than I would have left him long ago. He's a drunk. He's drunk now. I know he is. He wouldn't have done this otherwise.'

'Not a drop has passed the man's lips this night,' O'Hara said firmly, and then he remembered that he had sold the sailor rum in the saloon; but it seemed wiser to say no more.

She gave him a savage glance. 'It's a lie. He must have got it somewhere else.'

'He was sober,' Gerard said.

And Spanish added, 'Sober as a judge.'

'That's right,' she said, weeping, 'now turn on me, as if you hadn't done enough. Why are you all starting on me? What have I done?' The tears smarted in the cuts in her lips and she fingered her mouth tenderly while she spoke. 'What's to become of me?' she asked. But the question was rhetorical and nobody answered.

They all heard the distant shot.

AND three minutes after Elwes left the harbour the boarding party arrived at the gate. Sergeant Barnaby, who was marching in rear so that he might more easily adjust his step to accommodate his length of leg, halted the party there and they fell out and lit cigarettes in the dark, leaning against the wall waiting for the Adjutant. The cigarettes glowed in the wind.

The Adjutant was punctual.

'Get fell in,' Sergeant Barnaby ordered.

They shuffled into file and followed the Adjutant along the quayside, marching along the track by the rails, to the head of the steps, and halted. The Adjutant counted them and then said,

'Pay attention. And listen carefully. As you have probably been told already, or if you haven't you should have been, we are going to board the *Ur of the Chaldees*. That's the ship that is anchored just now in the middle of the harbour. You've all seen the ship and know roughly what she looks like. Some of you may have been on it. You can't mistake it, even in the dark. All right, then. First, how do we get there? Well, that's simple enough: in a boat; it's lying at the foot of the steps here, or should be. How do we get on board? That's not difficult either; there's a gangway hanging down the side. When we do get on board, don't run about on your own. Wait for orders. In amphibious operations discipline is, if anything, even more important than in ordinary land operations. Bear that in mind. Is that clear so far? How many of you can row?'

Nobody answered.

154

'Nobody.' He seemed a little discouraged. 'Well, it's very easy. Don't be afraid of it, that's all. Don't try and rush things. Sergeant, you will take the bows. That's the sharp end of the boat, in case you don't know. Then you.' He laid a hand on the man's shoulder. 'Then you. You will row. Then you and you. You also will row. If there are six oars, then each man will have one. Anyway, that's the order in which you will board. I shall take the stern and steer. Is that understood?'

Nobody spoke.

'One word more. This will be your first experience of amphibious operations. We shall be doing quite a lot of them one day, when we go back to France. So learn, learn all you can while you can. Incidentally there'll be no smoking or talking. Any questions?'

Nobody had any questions to ask.

'Very well. Sergeant, I shall need you. Come with me.'

Together they went down the steps to the sea.

'Got your flashlight?'

'No, sir.'

The Adjutant turned to him in the dark. 'D'you mean to tell me you've embarked on an operation of this nature without a flashlight, Sergeant?'

'Thought you'd have one, sir,' said Barnaby sullenly.

'You've got to learn to rely on yourself, man,' the Adjutant told him testily — 'that is the first prerequisite of the junior commander. Read your *Infantry Training*. I can't see a damn thing.'

'I never thought, sir.'

155

'That is a piece of redundant information, Sergeant.' He struck a match, whose minute flame died instantly in the wind, but in its brief spark he saw the outline of the grey-back in the sea at the foot of the steps. 'There it is. Get the men. And don't make much noise.'

Timidly into the pit of the night they followed the N.C.O. down the steps, against whose flat surfaces little seas flung themselves and tossed jets of frosted spume into the faces of the men climbing unsteadily into the boat. Sergeant Barnaby was first, the others followed him.

'How many oars are there, Sergeant?'

'Don't know, sir.'

'Well, find out. For God's sake try and be a little less helpless.'

'I don't see, sir.'

'Feel, then. If you'd brought a flashlight all this nonsense would have been avoided.' He cast off and climbed into the boat, taking his place in the stern, and found the smooth wet tiller.

'There's four, sir, I think.' There was a note of alarm in his voice as the boat drifted away from the steps into the bristling swell.

'Get them out, then, and hurry.'

The men struggled with the heavy oars in the boat to get them into the rowlocks and the frost on the oars numbed their fingers.

'Don't pull till I give the word,' the Adjutant ordered, 'then all pull together. Take the time from me. Are you all ready?'

A man said, 'No, sir,' and sounded on the verge of tears. 'Who's that?'

'Me, sir. Humphries. Can't find the rowlock, sir.'

The Adjutant said, 'Find it for him, Barnaby,' with bitter patience.

The blade struck the sea. 'All right, sir; I got it.'

'Are you all ready, then?'

He compressed his lips to give the word. He knew it was too late to withdraw now. He knew that what he was doing was arrant folly, a piece of dangerous stupidity without a redeeming feature. In his heart he was afraid. You could not see where it might end. He should command them now to turn about and row back to the steps and moor the boat and get out and march home and go back to bed. And yet! He turned it over in his mind. It might succeed. It might. There was always the lovely possibility of success, of a triumph so complete that . . . and there was the greater likelihood of galling defeat, of failure, and of the Commanding Officer's unmoved acceptance of his defeat, the open laughter of the people and the wordless derision of the Company Commander. But that would have to be outfaced anyway.

'Pull!' he said.

The oars bit deeply, too deeply, into the water.

'Pull!' he shouted. 'One . . . two, one . . . two.'

Wildly now the trembling soldiers tugged at their oars, and each time the blades struck the sea a shower of spray fell across the officer's face. The boat slowly gathered way.

'Speed it up,' the Adjutant commanded. 'Faster. Don't go

so deep with your oars.' He could see the white caps of the waves now and the gleaming foam where the oars stabbed the water; over the heads of the crew he peered into the darkness. Suddenly one of the men caught his breath sharply and there was a splash and the confused clatter of a body falling heavily into the bilge. A man laughed and silenced himself abruptly.

'What's the matter?'

'It's 'Umphries, sir.'

''E's lost 'is oar.'

The Adjutant whispered, 'Dear God!'

Humphries said, 'Missed the bloody sea, sir. Fell backwards and lost me oar. The bastard slipped out of me 'and.' He was near to tears.

The Adjutant called to Sergeant Barnaby, but there was no reply. The boat lost way somewhat and it was hard for the officer to adjust the rudder so as to counteract the loss of the oar, and the boat rose and plunged and the bilge-water ran splashing to and fro and from side to side among the straining feet.

'Humphries!'

'Yes, sir?'

'Report to me when we get back.'

'Yes, sir.'

'Sergeant Barnaby!'

In the bows he heard faintly a muffled retching. He remembered then that he had heard the sound for two or three minutes.

'The Sergeant's puking 'is 'eart out, sir.'

As and when his stomach revolted, the Sergeant vomited, lolling his head over the gunwale till the waves rose and mercifully washed his face and the tears of bile from his eyes; he did not hear the Adjutant calling.

'Keep going,' the Adjutant said. 'One . . . two, one . . . two!' After a while he relapsed into silence.

Then the boat struck the great wall of the northern jetty and Humphries fell backwards off his seat again and there was a great scuffling in the bilge. The Adjutant shouted to them to fend off, fend off with their oars, as the boat ground against the concrete. Above, the rim of the jetty loomed against the sky. They shoved the heaving thing away from the jetty.

'Now we know where we are,' the Adjutant said, and bitterly, 'that's something to be thankful for.'

He steered towards the middle of the harbour and they rowed steadily for a few minutes. We should be somewhere near it now, he thought to himself, and strained his eyes and ears into the unanswering void. He could see nothing. There was no deeper darkness, no heavier bulk against the sky.

'Humphries!'

'Yes, sir?'

'You're doing nothing. Bail.'

'What with, sir?' the soldier asked wretchedly.

'Anything. Improvise, man. Use your helmet.'

The soldier took off his helmet and scooped blindly in the bilge and tossed the water over the side.

'Are you throwing that at me?' the Adjutant demanded immediately.

'No, sir.'

'Well, be more careful. You're in trouble enough already.'

Sergeant Barnaby retched mournfully in the bows.

'All right, stop rowing.'

He strained into the infinite tumult of the sea. Holding the tiller under his arm, he gathered a little bunch of matches in his fingers and struck them so that they caught fire simultaneously and raised the flare above his head. In the bright light it gave the white faces of the crew ogled at him and the tossing waves leapt up at him out of the well of the sea and the oars were like long white legs on either side. He saw nothing else, and when the flame died the maddening yellow shapes drifted up over his eyes.

But on the quayside Winslow saw the spark of light. Already he was nervous, for he had been alone a long time and had heard once or twice what he had thought was a voice whose source he could not identify. He raised his rifle. Should he open fire? He could not be wrong in doing so. He brought the butt to his shoulder and aiming a little above where the light had been, he pressed the trigger.

The bullet passed whispering over the Adjutant's head and struck the wall of the northern jetty near the sea low down among the weeds and flattened itself noisily. Winslow heard the answering cry and fired again, and this time the bullet seemed to pass between the heads of the oarsmen; it ricochetted from the sea and bounced over the jetty, sighing in the wind.

The Adjutant shouted, 'Stop firing!' with a note of panic in his voice. 'Stop firing!'

The soldiers rested on their oars with heads nervously lowered and the sergeant vomited wearily over the gunwale.

'Stop firing!' He waited. 'Can you hear me?' The wind caught his voice and flung it away into the sky. 'Friends!' he screamed — 'friends!' His voice broke and he cursed with the fury of impotence. The sentries had not been warned, that was what it was; they had not been told of the operation. Somebody might have been killed, might easily; almost he wished it had indeed happened, so that the heinousness of the omission might be brought home the more fully to the responsible party — Gerard obviously. Typical. Negligence of the worst possible genre. Now they would have to return to the shore. Now the whole expedition was stillborn. To go on with the search for the ship, to go on rowing about the harbour in the dark, striking matches looking for a ship, under the fire of one's own men — no, it was unthinkable. He swung the tiller over and commanded the men to row. It was a pity the operation had to be cancelled for such a reason.

When they reached the steps at last — and it took a long time — and moored the boat there, the Adjutant left the seven men, ordering them to return to their billets, and set off down the quayside towards the guard-house. The men assisted Sergeant Barnaby up the steps and began the long walk home. They did not speak to one another.

★

'How much longer?' she asked in a whisper.

It would not be long now, Spanish said.

'I can't stand it much longer.'

The ship was slow now, Spanish told her; the keel had weed on it as long as a girl's hair — longer.

She held up a finger. 'Listen.'

'No need to listen.'

'Why doesn't it come?'

Gerard said, 'Be patient, it will,' and she threw him a venomous glance.

'It'll shake the house,' Spanish remarked.

'He must have been drunk,' she muttered. 'He wouldn't have left me like this. There must have been some reason, if he wasn't drunk.'

'He'd never have got her out of the harbour,' Spanish said. 'He must have slipped the anchor. That's not easy at the best of times.'

'I don't understand it. I never did anything that wasn't for his own good.'

O'Hara had left them and gone into the saloon to get a little brandy. He had a bottle of Henessey, he said, kept for just such an occasion. Now he returned carrying the two glasses, one for her and one for himself, Spanish and Gerard having refused. 'There,' he said, giving her the liquor, 'that'll make you feel better.'

'Thank you, Uncle. Dear Uncle!'

He paused with the glass at his lips. 'Yes.' He seemed to weigh the endearment. 'That's what a lot of people say. Well, chin up.' He drank. 'We'll have a lovely service of commemoration, on the jetty there, where the old ship was moored, with the choir, and cast a wreath upon the waters.'

'Thank you, dear.' She sipped the brandy; it stung her lips again and she frowned.

Suddenly Allan Gerard spoke. 'Why doesn't the damned ship blow up and get this over?' he demanded.

'It's a long way to Oran,' Spanish said.

'What?' Hilda Thwaite looked at him. 'What did you say? Oran?'

'Yes.' He was surprised.

'What do you know about it? Why did he say that?' She knew instinctively that it was important.

The Harbour Commissioner shrugged his shoulders. 'I don't know, except that we were talking a bit about Oran and places. Nothing particular. I never went there myself.'

'Why?' she insisted — 'why that place? What was he saying about it?'

Exceedingly uncomfortable, Spanish hesitated. 'Oh, he was saying he once knew a bit of a girl there, years ago.'

Now she rose, smiling a little, triumph in her widening eyes. 'So that's it. I knew there was a reason. I knew, I knew. I knew if he wasn't drunk there was something. A girl.' She laughed aloud. 'Another woman. What else did he say?'

'It was nowt, Mrs. Thwaite.' He was somewhat alarmed. 'A bit of a dream. He'd forgotten about it till we started talking.'

'He hadn't,' she said, 'he hadn't. What sort of a girl?'

'Portuguese,' he said.

'A foreigner.' She addressed Allan Gerard, throwing her words at the mockery in his eyes. 'I might have guessed. Some dirty little tart he picked up while he was away from home. Now he's gone back to her, has he? and left me. That's why he left me, isn't it? For her. Isn't it?'

'Nonsense,' Allan Gerard said.

'Yes, it is. I knew he couldn't leave me for nothing.' She smiled at the soldier. 'Now you see.'

'Be brave,' he said.

She turned to the Irishman. 'Uncle O'Hara, you under-stand, don't you?' And then to Spanish, 'You do.'

'Sure,' O'Hara answered heartily, 'we all understand.'

She thanked him again. 'It's you and I now,' she said.

'In what way would you be meanin', Mrs. Thwaite?' he asked her gently.

'You and I,' she said, 'against the world.'

'I'm very busy with the choir just now,' he began, clear-ing his throat, 'and one thing or another. The hotel keeps me runnin' from mornin' till night. Naturally I'll be glad to do anything a friend can.'

Hilda Thwaite raised her eyebrows; she waited, for he seemed to be about to speak again.

'Anything a friend can, naturally,' he repeated.

'If I thought it would do the least bit of good,' Allan Gerard said quietly, 'if I thought it would have the slightest effect, I would try and explain to you the elements of common decency, Mrs. Thwaite.' He knew it would serve no purpose, but he went on, 'Somewhere out on the sea there, that wretched old man you've hounded for the last twenty years is driving his ship into the minefield. Try and hold your peace until then, will you? When it happens, I hope I may be the first to congratulate you, you and Uncle O'Hara both. I imagine the old man had something of the sort in mind for you.'

But the Irishman interrupted. 'One moment, Captain . . .'

He stopped speaking, however, when he met the soldier's eyes. Allan Gerard was thinking what a pleasant thing it was to think of.

★

THE Adjutant was not challenged until he had passed the guard-house, in whose window the yellow light shone like an unsleeping eye, and he had already left the rails.

'Who's that?' he asked immediately of the sentry. 'This is the Adjutant.'

'Advance and be recognized.'

He went nearer to the dark figure. 'Who are you?' he asked. 'What's your name?'

'Winslow, sir.' He lowered the point of his bayonet reluctantly.

'Did you fire into the harbour just now?'

'Yes, sir.'

'Why?'

''Ow was I to know who it was, sir?'

'That wasn't what I asked you. Hadn't you been warned? Didn't you know there'd be a boat in the harbour tonight?'

'No, sir.'

'I see.' He was not surprised. 'Well, you're a rotten shot, that's all I can say.'

Winslow said he had not been shooting to kill.

'Then why were you shooting at all?'

Winslow moistened his lips. 'As a warning, sir.'

The Adjutant said, 'What the hell is the use of a warning? The Boche won't wait for warnings. Next time, shoot to kill.'

'Yes, sir.'

'Where's the other sentry?'

Winslow did not reply. This was the question he had feared and for which he had no reply other than that which was true.

'Well, where is he?'

'On patrol, sir.' He felt better. 'Prowling,' he added, elaborating the lie.

'You're lying. Aren't you?'

He was silent.

'Yes, you are. Where is he? Tell the truth, man.'

'Prowling, sir.'

'What d'you mean, prowling? Sentries work in pairs, don't they? Don't they? Why isn't he with you?'

'Don't know, sir. In the closet,' he said suddenly.

'You're lying again, Winslow. We'll see about this. Come with me.'

As he turned, Elwes came out of the darkness running.

He halted, his breath visible in the wind. 'Winslow?' he said — 'is that you, Winslow?'

The Adjutant said, 'Where have you been?'

Elwes stiffened, recognizing the voice. He swallowed. 'He was in the closet, sir,' said Winslow quickly.

'Shut up, you,' the Adjutant ordered him, and then to Elwes, 'Where have you been? Well?' He waited. 'Come along, man, I can't wait here all night.'

It was useless to lie, easy and quite useless. The officer could discover the truth sooner or later, and anyway he suddenly had no desire to lie, for the exhilaration of the music he had played on an instrument scarcely capable of a pure note made him careless of any consequences and the humiliation of discovery was always intolerable.

'I deserted my post, sir,' he said deliberately.

'Oh, you did.'

'Yes, sir. Wasn't Winslow's fault.'

'Where did you go?'

'In a fisherman's cottage.'

'That's very interesting. In a fisherman's cottage. What's your name?'

'Elwes, sir.'

The Adjutant said, 'Aren't you the man who played the fiddle on the jetty this afternoon?'

'Yes, sir.'

'Yes, I thought so. What were you doing in a fisherman's cottage?'

'I was playing the violin.'

'I see. One of these days, Elwes, you may have the opportunity of playing the fiddle to a German, a good big one, who will be holding a bayonet.'

Elwes did not speak.

'Follow me, Elwes.'

The soldier shouldered his rifle and followed the Adjutant down the jetty to the guard-house, whose door the officer threw open. Corporal Foster, who was sitting at the table reading in the light of the hurricane-lamp, looked up startled.

'Corporal Foster.'

'Yes, sir.' He got to his feet slowly.

'Place this man under close arrest.'

Corporal Foster looked at Elwes, who avoided his glance, his head turning away. 'Yes, sir,' he said.

'Have you any handcuffs?'

'No, sir.'

'He must be watched, then. He must not be left alone, do you understand? Bad type. Dangerous.'

THEY had forgotten him. In the parlour it was warm and exclusive and there was much between them; they had forgotten the Adjutant. They were very surprised, therefore, when he came in and stood in the doorway, looking from one to the other. His uniform was wet and there was water on his glasses, and on his sleeve, alive like a glow-worm in the flickering firelight, a shred of seaweed. His face was white and he seemed to be trembling. He drew off his gloves, one finger after the other.

Spanish broke the silence diffidently. 'You've come back,' he said.

His voice, when he spoke, was low, almost a whisper. 'Where is the *Ur of the Chaldees?*'

'Isn't she there?' Spanish miserably asked him.

'Kindly answer my question.'

So the Harbour Commissioner said, 'She sailed.'

'Yes . . . where to?'

Spanish said he did not know.

'Oran,' Hilda Thwaite answered bitterly, 'for a Portu-guese tart.'

'He's sailed the blockship into the minefield, hasn't he?'

They did not speak.

'Damn a man who sinks his own ship!'

They waited, the words living for a moment in the little room, looking for a way out. When the door opened again, they turned simultaneously towards it as though expecting it would be Daniel Thwaite, but it was not; Alexander Perry came in timidly, fumbling in his pockets, and went to the centre of the room where the light was brightest.

'Now, has everybody got a lucky charm?' he asked.

Only Allan Gerard laughed.

'Because I have a fresh supply. For example.' He held out his hand, full of the little charms, and selecting those he favoured, began, 'I have a very interesting line in giraffes. Curious fellows. They say a giraffe can balance a glass of water on its head when trotting. Monkeys . . . hear no evil, speak no evil, see no evil. A rhinoceros. Notice the shortness of the tail for so large a body. Found in Central Africa. Then — ah, yes, a quaint little chap — the mandrill. The colouring is quite remarkable. Their faces are red and their hands are blue, and they put to sea in a sieve. Like the Jumblies. A very great poet, Edward Lear, whose importance is underestimated.' He extended his hand. 'Would any gentleman care for one?'

Nobody spoke.

'It is an offer I shall not be able to repeat.'

They looked away.

'All you need is faith . . .'

He offered the charms to each in turn. 'No?'

He shook his head and put the things back into his pocket and went into the saloon slowly.

Hilda Thwaite held up her finger. 'Sh!'

The Adjutant had been about to speak, but her gesture silenced him. He began again, 'I'm tired of this shilly-shallying. You knew all about this, Spanish, didn't you? You were well aware that Captain Thwaite had every intention of taking his ship out of the harbour tonight, weren't you? Answer me. I'm trying to keep my temper. And yet you forebore to warn me, knowing that I was going to attempt to board the ship to-night; you allowed me in cold blood to embark upon an amphibious operation with half a dozen idiots whose incompetence was a danger to themselves and to me. How is it the ship's disappearance coincided so damned exactly with my arrival? Because you told the Captain, didn't you?'

'I won't be your scapegoat, mister,' Spanish said stolidly.

'Did you tell him or didn't you?'

'He didn't require telling. He knew well enough what was coming. He wasn't going to let you put soldiers on his ship.'

The Adjutant turned to the Company Commander. 'And you, Gerard, why do you think he sailed? As if I give a solitary damn.'

Gerard suggested, 'Let it drop, Billy, you've done enough.'

'Where's the sentry — your sentry?'

Gerard looked up sharply. 'They're on duty.'

'They're not. One of them deserted his post. I have placed him under close arrest. It's Elwes. He's in the guardroom.'

Gerard stared at him expressionlessly. Then he picked up his cap from the desk and went out without a word.

They went, then, down to the quayside, where there were already many others, and stood in the bitter darkness, their eyes turned towards the sea, which was invisible; a monstrous, nameless bulk that lisped among the weeds growing out of the concrete. Here the wind was not so strong. They huddled together under the frost and waited. Hilda was among them and did not know exactly why, and O'Hara, he having little choice, at her side; and the verger, the mechanic, and the man from the reservoir; Gilderson, Peter Williams, the wives of the fishermen;

and many others; all waiting for the explosion. When it came, there would be a burst of conversation, and men would light cigarettes. They would go home, then, satisfied.

★

THE Chief Engineer came up from the engine-room to the bridge and stood beside the old man there in the violent darkness and found the proximity of death exhilarating, for it was in the shop already.

He shouted, 'Mind if I sing a note or two?'

When Captain Thwaite said no, he did not mind if the engineer sang at all, the engineer opened his mouth and sounded his voice with a tonic sol-fa and then started to sing, throwing back his head so that the long hair flew in the wind, singing lustily. The old man at his side took little notice. He peered into the darkness, not knowing what he sought there, but narrowing his eyes into it perhaps from force of habit, perhaps against the explosion when it would come, and each time the frightened vessel rose and hung sickeningly on the fulcrum of a wave and the propeller panicked foolishly, giddily, under her stern, he gripped the rail to help her, waiting with his breath held for the plunge into the trough where the mine might lie. The beams strained and wept aloud to the limit of endurance, surely, and then beyond, achingly and dreadfully, and in the wheelhouse the bottles rolled to and fro and the doors banged.

Then the old man remembered the machine-gun in the bows. He left the bridge and went down and forward, lurching against the lurching of the ship. He pulled the butt of the gun into the hollow of his shoulder and braced himself and pressed the trigger and the dizzying flashes lit the deck and he wanted badly to shout, to shout anything, deliriously, and so did: diffident profanities, because there was nothing coherent in his mind at that time. The gun slithered across the streaming deck with the vibration and his body vibrated also because he was a part of the gun, which is the way to fire a gun, and a part of the smoothly sliding lock and the charge and the slowly scarlet-turning tracer that circled lazily over the sky. With a deep-chested roar the sea cuffed the blunt stem of the ship and the steeple of spray that leapt the rearing bows and fell hissing across the boards and drenched him, these were a part of him also at that moment. He fired again and the hot cases rolled into the scuppers and the barrel steamed. On the bridge the Chief Engineer thought to himself, That gun will seize if he is not very careful. Lewis guns seize, he remembered, easily; he ought to keep it down to bursts of four or five rounds.

The sentry on the southern jetty saw the great white flash in the dawn and heard the distant rumble a moment later. Watson West, the fisherman who was heading for the open sea from the beach, saw it; and those waiting on the quayside. The old ship came down on the mine in the slough between two great waves and the explosion lifted her high out of the water and broke her back. She sank almost at once, and when she went down the machine-gun was still firing in the bows.

THE soldiers fell silent when Agnes entered the guard-house on the quayside. There were only three or four of them, but the hurricane-lamp on the table threw their shadows on the walls so that the little place seemed unbearably crowded and the light shone below the level of the faces turned towards her and gave them terrible hostility, and she paused. Elwes was sitting, she saw, on the bench at the table.

Corporal Foster asked her what she wanted there.

'I want to speak to Fred Elwes,' she said, 'please.' She was frightened and could not keep it from her voice.

Corporal Foster hesitated; then he motioned to the rest and they followed him out. When the door was closed she drew breath.

'Frederick Elwes.'

'Hello, Agnes,' he said sheepishly. He did not look at the girl.

'The Harbour Commissioner told me summat was wrong.' She paused. 'What is it?'

'Nothing.' His hands lay along his knees and he stared at the stove in the middle of the hut.

'Yes, there is.'

'No, there's not, Agnes.'

'What have you been doing?' She spoke as one would to a child. 'You can't hide anything from me.'

'I haven't been doing anything, Agnes.'

Now she was thoroughly alarmed. 'You're telling lies,' she told him. 'You've been up to some mischief.'

Impatiently he threw off the influence she was trying to exert over him. 'Run along, Agnes, there's a good lass. The Captain will be here in a minute.'

'You're in trouble.' Her voice softened and she moved towards him involuntarily. 'Frederick Elwes . . . Fred, tell me, what's wrong?'

He raised his head; her face was real and mobile in the firelight and her eyes were shining; he looked away quickly. 'It's nowt,' he said, 'nowt. You ought to be in bed, lass, at this time of night. You're looking a bit tired.'

'I'll know sooner or later, so you may as well tell me now.'

'Go to bed and get some sleep.'

'Oh, Fred, Fred'— she wrung her hands —'summat terrible has happened. What is it? Tell me.'

'It's not of the least importance.' He was a little irritated.

'I'll be the judge of that,' she retorted.

'Very well.' He let out the breath slowly. 'I wasn't on duty when the ship went,' he said heavily, 'and I should have been.' The fire glowed immensely in his eyes. 'It's nothing to worry about — a bit of punishment, that's all it'll be.'

'Fred, I don't understand.'

'I deserted my post,' he said.

Her hand went to her open mouth. She said, 'I told you, didn't I? I told you to be careful of that ship. Frederick Elwes, you won't take a telling, will you? I warned you.'

'Yes, Agnes.'

'What are they going to do to you?'

'I don't know. Some sort of a court-martial, I suppose.'

She cried, aghast, 'They'll execute you.'

'Don't be so daft, lass,' he told her impatiently. 'A month or two in jail, that's all it'll be.'

'I could kill you,' she said furiously. 'If I ever forgive you for this . . .'

'It's nothing, I keep telling you.'

'I'll talk to the Captain,' she cried; 'I'll show him. I'll give him court-martial.'

'You'll do nowt o' t' sort.'

'Why did you have to do it? Oh, Fred'— she dropped on her knees at his side —'don't you understand anything?'

He looked down at her face. There were tears in her eyes and the red hands, where they lay in her lap, trembled. He looked away hastily, inarticulate with embarrassment.

'Gurt fool,' she whispered.

'It's my funeral,' he muttered.

''Tis as much mine as thine, lad.'

'Get up off your knees, girl; you'll get cramp or else.'

'I won't.' She shook her head. 'For that's where I am to thee, Fred, and that's where I'll stay.'

His eyes drifted to her hair and he stretched out his hand timidly to touch it. 'Your hair's pretty in the light," he said.

'Is it?'

He swallowed. 'What are you looking like that for?'

"I love you, Fred,' she whispered. 'Somebody's got to say it, one or the other, and so I said it, for you never would.'

'Don't cry.' He could think of nothing else to say at that moment. He was much embarrassed; the thing was over-whelming; he did not know what he thought. 'Don't cry,' he said.

'I could brain you for it.' She put a hand on his arm and shook it. 'If only I'd seen you, I'd have stopped you going; you'd never have gone.' She hesitated suddenly. 'Where did you go?'

'The fisherman's. He wanted me to go and play for him and his wife. He couldn't manage any other time.'

'Ey, dear, just for that! I'd have stopped you all right. I'd have been able to tell — there's nothing you can hide from me.' She added emphatically, 'So don't ever try, Frederick Elwes, never all your life, never try to do any-thing behind your wife's back.'

And he said shyly, 'You talk as though we were going to be wedded.'

'For goodness' sake, man, what d'you think I've been saying for the last five minutes?' she said.

He smiled and the smile remained fixed on his face. He thought maybe he ought to be smiling; but his heart was not at ease. It seemed a little rapid. A decision had been made about him and he had had no part in it. But it was a lovely thing, surely. It was so marvellous a thing that he could not think what it was that was wrong with it, that gave him this feeling of . . . well? he asked himself, what feeling? It was nameless. It needed considerable thought. And he had not had the time or the solitude. 'I hadn't thought about that,' he said.

'Then you'd better start thinking,' she said, 'for if I let you take your own time about it you'd take fifty years or more.'

'There's plenty of time, Agnes.'

'Don't you want to, then?' She rose from her knees.

'I'm greatly honoured,' he said, 'but . . .'

'You're not hiding something from me, are you?'

He knew instinctively that she would not understand what he would say, but there was no other answer. 'There's a lot to be done. Me, I mean; I've a lot to do. I wasn't thinking of getting wed just yet. I don't know enough, not enough about anything. We haven't done much walking out, have we?'

'You don't love me,' she said.

'Yes, I do.'

'You don't, or you couldn't say such things.'

He said miserably, 'There's a lot I wanted to do when the war's over.'

'You need someone to look after you,' she told him. 'That's what you need, someone to see you don't get into mischief. Look at you now, going to be court-martialled or some such nonsense. Perhaps you'll ask me first in future.'

'I'd have done it just the same, Agnes,' he said gently.

'Frederick Elwes!' she exclaimed, 'I believe you're a thoroughly bad man.'

He added slyly, 'The court-martial will teach me, though.'

Her brittle anger broke and she softened again. 'Oh, Fred, how long will it be?'

'Don't cry, don't cry. Don't you worry.'

'I'll be waiting for you,' she said, 'no matter how long.' And she added, again with the curiously menacing severity that now amused and attracted him, 'Remember, now.'

But he did not understand the unease deep in his stomach.. In the dark she passed the Company Commander and went back to the inn to her room in the roof, where she lay on the bed weeping for a long time, for she had found her love and it was slipping out of her grip before she could mould it and fasten it to herself. Below her, in the room beneath, she heard a woman talking excitedly to herself, or maybe she was addressing some imaginary person, for there was no reply.

HE KNEW the Company Commander would come as soon as he was told of the arrest. He dreaded it. He prayed that Gerard would rate him, lacerate him verbally, knowing well that Gerard would not, and Allan Gerard's silence would be hard to bear indeed; this would be his punishment, a scourge beside which any sentence the court might pronounce would be a mockery. He rose when the officer entered the little place and turned his head away and his eyes to the corner of the hut where there was no light, and waited.

'Sit down.'

He sank on to the bench again. The officer lit a cigarette and stood above the stove looking down at the open grate whence the bright glow flooded the dusty floor and his boots.

'That girl,' Allan Gerard began. He paused. 'Bit young, aren't you?'

'Yes, sir,' he whispered.

'You make up your own mind.'

He was silent then for a long time. The sweat broke out in the palms of the soldier's hands and left imprints on the dry bench; he waited, counting the pulse in his ears; the fire roared and the wind buffeted the chimney till the soot fell and the flames were a gay blue colour for a moment.

'I'm sorry, sir,' he blurted at last.

Gerard threw his cigarette into the fire. 'Why did you do it, Elwes? For God's sake, why?'

That was what Corporal Foster had said, Elwes thought.

'You had only to ask — ask me, ask Foster. Foster's a good fellow; he would have arranged a stand-in for you for an hour if you wanted to go.'

Corporal Foster had said that also, and it was true.

'Well, why?'

He said at last, 'I'd have to tell him.'

'Where you were going, you mean? and what for?'

Yes, he supposed that was the reason; but it was something more than that: it sprang from that and grew away from it to a nameless instinct, an overwhelming revulsion to acknowledge his identity until he was certain . . . no, you could not go on with it and hope that a handful of words would clothe a naked sensation like that.

'Elwes, you've got to learn to brazen it out with yourself as well as with everybody else. It'll cause you wretchedness all your life if you don't. What I can't understand is why you didn't ask me — me particularly.' He faced the soldier. 'Dear God, man, you make me think I've failed in everything I've tried to do. Are you afraid of me?'

Elwes raised his eyes now, in surprise.

'Do the other men think that, too?' Gerard said.

'We'd do any mortal thing for you,' he replied gravely.

Much embarrassed, the Company Commander said, 'Damn it all, that isn't what I meant, man.'

'I'm sorry,' the wretched soldier repeated, 'I'm sorry, sir, to have caused so much trouble.'

'Oh, it's yours, Elwes. You'll get anything up to six months' detention and there's nothing I can do to help you — nothing at all.'

Elwes said six months was a long time.

'Depends how you look at it.' He paused and then, with a deliberate change of the pitch of his voice, said, 'Elwes, there's something I want to say to you. It's been on the tip of my tongue for some time and I have been trying to think of the best way of saying it so that you'll understand fully.'

He pulled the decrepit wooden chair over and sat across it on the other side of the fire. 'This court-martial, Elwes . . it isn't important to you. It doesn't matter. That's the thing you've got to remember. It's you, d'you see? — you who are important. You are vital, absolutely vital. I want to impress that on you so that you never forget. Right now you are the most important person in the world. For you are greatly needed. Much is expected of you in exchange for nothing given except jealousy and enmity and laughter. You are the hope of mankind and the rising sun. If you are hated, glory in it, because it will mean that you will become a force, a great cleansing flame. I wish I could help you, give you a little advice or something, so that you would not have to start from nothing. All I know is a little of what not to do, for I wouldn't accept my responsibilities. Very few of us do. We duck our obligations and postpone the day of reckoning for the shabby peace and quiet that gets you here, in this place, in a uniform, all trussed up like a chicken for the roasting. I tried and I failed. I never really tried. There are millions like me, Elwes, born in one war and killed in another, running to and fro between these two catastrophes, unable to go further back than the last one, nor further forward than the next, like trapped mice.' He stopped suddenly. 'You do understand, don't you? All this isn't being wasted on you, is it?' he asked the soldier, whose eyes were riveted on his face.

'Yes, sir.'

He continued, 'Because it's urgent now, and if you don't understand, if you put it off because it isn't clear to you, you won't win the war or anything else, ever. Accept your responsibilities, even though you don't know what they are. Go and look for them. Don't wait. And don't think that because you're the only one, you're all alone. Don't let them stop you. They'll try, they'll do every damned thing they can to stop you. You'll have a rotten time. Everything lousy that ever happened to anybody will happen to you. Take it, take the whole bloody issue. I can't even tell you what it is you'll be looking for. An idea, that's all it is, something stirring in the souls of men at last. The blessed realisation at last that alone you are less than nothing, that your life is part of the life of the man next door and in the next street and the next city and state. Try Coventry and London and Hull and Rotterdam and Norway and France and even Germany . . . that's the sort of place you'll find it. The flower that blossoms in the pit — that's as near as I can get to it. Just keep on, and one day you'll see it, the whole fantastic thing, and it will have been worth it, worth all the centuries of misery you've been through and all those still to come. And if you can't do anything with what I'm telling you, then give it to another man. You understand? Don't let it die. Remember that. Don't let it die in you. Remember.'

The soldier nodded.

THE TIMOROUS flutter of light preceded the sound of the explosion by several seconds. It was over and beyond the fisherman's own horizon, but this was near, for he was on the surface of the sea. He thought maybe it was gunnery practice or a convoy under attack out beyond the minefield, though he could not in fact hear aircraft in the sky, and to-morrow there would be a cap in the surf or a spar or something and flotsam on the beaches to the south. There might be salvage. He turned the high prow of his boat towards where the sound had come from; on the way he would cast the lines. The hot breath of the engine played pleasantly about his legs.

Codling brought a good price. He always fished primarily for codling, though he was glad of anything that took the bait. There were not many left, however; when you fish certain grounds and always the same grounds year in and year out, the fish leave and do not breed there after a time and you get only itinerant fish coming in with the tides or going south with the season. It is better to fish in different waters whenever possible, so that you can come back to the good ones. If, however, you have no choice, there being, for example, a minefield boxing you to a maximum troll of four or five miles, you go on fishing in the same places, seeing your catch diminish each month, and you are unable to help yourself because it is your living and you must go on destroying it.

He throttled down to a speed at which leeway was barely maintained and pinioned the tiller, and fastening the end of the first line to a float, he hurled the float far out over the side. Then he began to throw out the line, running it through his hands with the hooks flying round his naked arm in such a way that you would have expected them to bury themselves in the flesh. He fastened the end of the line to a dab, and then began the next line. It took a long time to cast seven trays of line, each being maybe two hundred yards long. When all the dabs were afloat, he left them and went on towards the minefield.

The dawn crept up the sky in the east and soon the pale green light covered him and sped towards the land. As he drew near to the minefield, he saw oil on the water, and farther on, a builder's plank; then there was a length of splintered wood and the break was white and clean and fresh; in a minute there was an old lifeboat scarcely afloat. He decreased speed and stood up in the stern to see better, and there was a corked bottle bouncing in the wake of his boat. Then there was a lot of wreckage, all together in one place, unidentifiable, and beyond it, maybe half a mile away, there was a man sitting on a raft over which the seas were breaking. He waved and the man waved. You could not tell whether the raft was in the minefield or not; on the edge, Watson West thought; he increased speed a little and narrowed his eyes and went into the minefield. He drew alongside the raft.

The man climbed stiffly into the boat. 'I'm obliged to you,' he said.

He was blue with cold. Watson West said, 'Better put my coat on. In the bows yonder. And sit on the engine-housing here; it's warm.' He put about. 'Likely to be any others?'

'No.' The man's teeth chattered uncontrollably.

At half speed, standing up in the stern to study the waters in his path, Watson West made for the shore. The man, who had the long hair of a hermit and a straggling grey beard, sat on the engine-housing in the coat.

'Drop of hot tea?' Watson West asked him. He gave the man the flask of tea Mrs. West had prepared for him and the man drank it slowly, holding the flask in both hands and letting the steam come up into his face.

'Did you hit a mine?'

'Yes.'

'What ship?'

'*Ur of the Chaldees.*' He sipped the tea.

Watson West said, 'What? What did you say?'

'*Ur of the Chaldees.* The blockship. Imbleness.'

'Where's the old man?'

'Went down with her. Must have done. I never saw him after the first minute. You one of the fishermen from Imble?' The beady eyes watched him over the rim of the flask.

'Yes. You must have sailed in the night, then.'

'We did.'

'You'll be the engineer.'

'Name of Edwards.'

'Mine's West.'

'Glad to meet you, mister.'

'How do you do.'

The engine hummed, and each time the little boat buried its stern in the troughs the exhaust outlet spat and choked and the fumes rose from the engine-housing.

'Didn't the old man know the minefield was there?'

'No.'

'Queer,' said Watson West in a moment. Then they were

silent. Over their heads the coming day explored the sky. The fisherman increased speed again, for he could see better now. They would be out of the minefield; he could see his floats rising and falling on the waves ahead of him.

'I've got my lines out,' the fisherman said.

'No hurry, mister.'

'Feeling better?'

Edwards nodded. 'There's your flask. Tea.'

'D'you mind if I take my lines in, Mr. Edwards, before we go back? It'll take a bit of time.'

'No hurry. I'll lend you a hand. The revolution won't be today.' The eyes did not move from the fisherman's face.

'Is there going to be one?'

'Certainly. What a question, I must say, coming from a member of the working classes.'

Watson West was somewhat embarrassed. He had never thought of himself as such; he was not sure, indeed, whether he was altogether pleased. 'As long as I can get my lines in,' he said lamely.

'I've been on strike this last year,' Edwards said. 'Come the seventeenth.'

'Yes. I heard about it.'

'Did you read my manifesto?'

'In the saloon, isn't it, in The Navigator, by the dart-board?'

'That's it.'

'Yes, I read it.'

'Workers of the world unite,' said the engineer with the air of one who casts a gauntlet.

Watson West felt embarrassed again. 'What for?' he asked. They were coming up to the last of the dabs he had thrown.

'What for? What against, you mean.'

'D'you mind taking the tiller a bit, Mr. Edwards?' he requested. 'It would make it a bit quicker and you'd keep warm against the engine. Keep her on the same course.' He throttled down till the boat lay wallowing in the swell and came alongside the first of the dabs that stretched away in a long straight line towards the land. He pulled it in and dropped it into the bilge. Then he began to take in the line. Each fish he threw into one of the boxes in the bows. There were not many, a few codling, flatfish, whiting, a bit of dog-fish. There were two crabs whose pincers had become tangled in the lines. The dying fish fluttered in the boxes and the crabs crawled restlessly in the bilge. A single gull hovered over the stern of the boat and uttered a sharp cry from time to time. He went on to the last floats. The sun was quite high in the sky when he had finished.

'All right,' he said at last; 'that's the lot.'

Edwards said, 'I said what against. Workers of the world unite what against.'

Watson West did not understand.

'You said unite what for, didn't you?' the engineer said patiently. 'Well, I said, what you mean is, what against.'

'I see.' The catch would bring maybe eighteen shillings, he thought.

'Against oppression, that's what against,' the engineer told him. He handed the tiller to the fisherman and returned to his seat on the engine-housing. 'Oppression of the people.'

'You've been reading newspapers, Mr. Edwards.'

'We've got to stand together. Remember that. Don't imagine because you saved my life I can forget my principles.'

Watson West was confused and irritated. He stared at the distant dunes. 'Mind I don't put you back on your raft,' he said at length.

'Go on, then. I'm ready.' The engineer rose from his seat on the engine-housing to emphasize his complete readiness, leaving the black moist imprint of his buttocks on the dry wood. 'Go on, then; put me back. I'm ready.'

'Sit down, Mr. Edwards.'

He did not want to talk. Now that he was on his way home it occurred to him suddenly to wonder what he would do when he got there. Yesterday he had sailed home knowing that in the afternoon he would look for and maybe find among the soldiers a man who could play the violin, and he had, and suddenly with a rush it was over, with a picture in his mind of Elwes in the firelight playing the instrument and Mrs. West crying a good deal because the sad music reminded her of Eunice, and there was a great empty space in his heart. He had begun the instrument for the child, and, her death notwithstanding, had finished it; you said about it, as you said about many things, Well, you might as well finish it now that it was begun; its completion had been in itself an objective; he had not projected his mind beyond that moment. And now it was achieved there was nothing to do. He had no desire to make anything else. You do not begin a thing simply to end it. He was going home and would auction the catch and have tea with his wife and then bait the hooks ready for tomorrow, and then, what?

THE CROWD had begun to gather on the beach as soon as Watson West's coble was sighted in the bay, for now the whole town knew that the blockship had sailed during the night and the sentry was under close arrest, having known indeed since a few moments after daylight, and it was reasonable to suppose the fisherman would have some news of the ship. When it was seen that the fisherman was not alone in his craft, their best expectations were realized and they crowded round the boat as it settled delicately on the cradle and helped to pull it out of the surf with much excited chatter and whispering about the silent man with long grey hair and brooding eyes who sat on the engine-housing and watched them. They drew the coble out of reach of the sea and Watson West climbed down the spokes of the great wheels and they waited for Edwards to follow the fisherman. He rose at length and with arms akimbo stared down at the little sea of faces. The people fell silent.

'Comrades,' he began.

'Better get down, Mr. Edwards,' said Watson West.

'Comrades.' He belched slightly, being very hungry.

'Comrades and ladies and gentlemen. In the struggle of
the working classes against capitalism and oppression generally, there rises from time to time a man who's made
an example of himself we ought to follow. Such a man was
Captain Daniel Thwaite, master of the *Ur of the Chaldees*,
sunk out there yonder in the minefield with all hands except
me, as we were marooned by the Admiralty here in Imbleness and left to rot with good turbines only needing
overhaul, and the hell with the owners too. That clique.'

The people gazed up at him.

Watson West said, 'We want to pull the boat up the
beach, Mr. Edwards.'

'Pull it up, then, pull it up. I'm not the man to interfere
with honest toil.' He continued, 'A martyr, comrades, that's
what Captain Thwaite was, a martyr to capitalist tom-
foolery. A victim to the military. The military is the tool of
capitalism.'

'Mr. Edwards, we can't pull the boat up the beach while
you're in it. We'd be obliged if you'd get out now.'

The crowd listened while the two men discussed the
matter. At length, reluctantly, the engineer descended from
the boat and pushed his way through the crowd. He walked
up the cobbled ramp towards the Harbour Commissioner's
office. In silence they watched him go, and when he was
out of sight they pulled the boat up the beach. One or two
followed the engineer.

Spanish was there, making tea. He looked up when the
engineer, not wholly unconscious of the drama latent in the
moment, made his entrance, and stared at the curious figure

outlined against the light, at first in open disbelief and then, as he recognized beneath the flowing hair and the beard the features of the man, somewhat reproachfully, the matter of the disappearance of the ship being complicated enough, Spanish considered, without survivors.

'I thought you were drowned,' he said.

'Well, I'm not,' the engineer retorted irritably, lifting the lid of the teapot and sniffing at the steam. 'Got anything to eat?'

'No. Better see Uncle O'Hara. Are there any more survivors?'

'The old man went down with her.'

Spanish tipped back his cap and rubbed his forehead wearily. 'This makes things even more difficult,' he said. 'Things were bad enough. Will you have a cup of tea?'

'I've just drunk a quart. I'm sick and tired of the stuff.'

'Aye, me too.' He poured himself a cup of tea. 'Poor old Thwaite. Twenty years or more, more, I knew him.'

'Martyred. Martyred, comrades.' The engineer stared out of the window. 'I've just been speaking to the crowds about the example he made of himself. Imagine me.'

'What did you say to them?'

'Everything, about how he'd given his life in the minefield for them and the proletariat and everything and how the working classes felt about it and ought to rise against oppression and one thing or another because of what the old man's gone and done. I told them. I was good, Spanish. They didn't give me time, but I got it in all right. He didn't die in vain.'

'There's no end to it, Mr. Edwards. Things just go from bad to worse.'

'I remember him marrying the woman,' the engineer said, 'I remember thinking at the time.'

Spanish sipped his tea. 'What else did you say?'

'Nothing particular. I could have said a lot.'

'You didn't mention I lent him the boat, did you?'

'No.'

'I'm glad you didn't mention that,' Spanish said, 'Thank God for that, anyway. There's no need ever to mention that.'

'That's true.'

'I don't know what will happen. Dear, oh dear! Things just get worse and worse.'

'There's going to be a revolution. There's got to be.'

'I meant about the blockship. Nothing ends because it's gone down. It might just as well still be there. Better, in fact. The military says there'll have to be another, that's all.' He poured himself another cup of tea. 'It makes you think what's the use.'

'You better not think about it, Spanish.'

'There's Maisie too.'

The engineer belched musically. 'I'm full of wind,' he said, tapping his stomach.

'What you need,' Spanish told him, 'is a bite to eat.'

'That's what I keep saying. And I got to write to the owners and tell them.'

'What about The Navigator? For a bite to eat?'

'Yes, that's right, I suppose.' He lowered his voice. 'While I think of it, by the way, talking about you lending the old man that boat, you needn't mention about me coming up once or twice when nobody was looking. During the stay-down strike, I mean. Make me look silly. You understand?'

'Naturally, naturally not.'

'That's it. Well, I'll be getting along now and see O'Hara, I think.'

'I'll walk along with you.'

While Edwards went towards the kitchen to find Uncle O'Hara, the Harbour Commissioner climbed the stairs and went along the dark corridor to the door of Hilda Thwaite's room and tapped on it. When he heard her voice he went in, taking off his cap.

He stood awkwardly by the door. 'The tidings is bad, Mrs. Thwaite,' he said. 'They're bad.'

She was sitting on the bed varnishing her nails and the room smelled sweetly of the varnish. Her eyes were red. She looked up at him and did not speak. Her lips, he saw in the light, were still bruised and swollen, and there was a cut on her cheek.

'It's bad news.'

She said at last, 'Well, what is it?'

'He's gone. He went down with her.' He moistened his lips. 'I'm sorry, Mrs. Thwaite. There's no good hoping. The engineer was saved, but the captain went down with her.' His voice trailed away.

She went on varnishing her nails. 'Thought as much,' she said.

'Everybody extends to you their deepest sympathy in your great bereavement.'

'The blasted fool!' Tears ran smoothly down her face. 'If there's ought I can do . . .'

She interrupted him. 'Yes. Keep your sympathy. Tell everybody to keep their sympathy.'

He was silent, fumbling with his cap.

'Get out,' she said. 'Go on, get out.'

Glad of release, he turned to leave.

'Listen!' She flared up suddenly. 'Don't think I'm crying because the old fool's dead. Don't get any wrong ideas. If he wasn't dead, I'd kill him anyway, for the way he's bilked me. Portuguese bitch!'

'Yes, m'm.' He wanted badly to get out of the room now.

'Well, he didn't. He didn't even do that. I'm getting married again, right away. Me and O'Hara. That's what we always planned. After the mourning. At St. Thomas's, with the choir.'

Spanish said, 'I must congratulate Uncle O'Hara.'

'He doesn't know yet. You shut up.'

'Oh!'

'That surprises you, doesn't it? Me and O'Hara.'

'Yes, m'm.'

'O'Hara's very fond of me.'

'Yes, he will be.'

She said impatiently, 'Oh, get out. It's no use talking to you.'

★

THE President was late. The Junior Member, who was a lieutenant, and the Senior Member, who was a captain, stood before the fire and warmed the calves of their legs and talked in low tones, the Junior Member asking many questions nervously, this being his first court-martial, the Senior Member answering them mostly as follows: 'You don't have to do or say anything at all, old boy. Just leave it to the President.' The Adjutant, who was the Prosecuting Officer, stared out of the window at the falling rain and watched the dead brown leaves fluttering down along the drive under the trees; he had laid his papers, the Summary of Evidence and the Statement as to Character and *King's Regulations* and the *Manual of Military Law*, on the table which the Court Orderly had prepared for him; like the other tables, of which there were two, his was covered with a grey blanket that smelled a little, he had noticed, of feet. The tables were arranged in such a way as to form three sides of a square, the large one being for the Court, the others being for the use of the Prosecuting Officer and the Defending Officer; on each table there was a rectangle of pink blotting-paper. In the fourth side of the square there was a chair standing alone. The Accused would sit there. Captain Gerard, who, by virtue of the accused man's request, was Defending Officer, studied his notes and smoked. Except for the three tables and the chairs, the room was quite naked. Footsteps were loud and harsh on the wooden floor. The windows rattled and a spider climbed slowly up the wall behind the President's chair.

On the other side of the door the Court Orderly, who

was the battalion Provost Sergeant, talked in a low voice to Corporal Foster, who was a witness and would give evidence if the Accused pleaded not guility. He had, of course, already testified in the Summary of Evidence. It was dark and cold in the corridor and you could feel the wind against your legs. They smoked furtively. Winslow stood beyond them, doing nothing, saying nothing, thinking nothing. And beyond Winslow the Accused stood at ease with his escort, these two being separated somewhat from the rest. Elwes listened to the sounds the wind made moving about the great dark house. It must be a very old house, he thought.

When the President arrived, the Provost Sergeant brought the little party to attention and saulted. Stand easy, he said when the officer had entered the room and closed the door.

The President said, 'Good morning, gentlemen.'

All the officers rose, looking at the President to see what what manner of a man he might be and whether he looked efficient and calm or slow and likely to fuss. He was a man of middle age; he was rotund and genial; he wore the Palestine medal; and he was extremely friendly.

'Hallo, Billy,' he greeted the Adjutant. 'I hear you're down for Staff College.'

'Down for it, sir, yes. Going to division for a bit first.'

'Lucky man.' He removed his cap and sat down at the President's table and opened his brief-case. 'Bloody cold in here.' He examined the papers. 'Now then, let's get this scallywag dealt with. I'm in a hell of a hurry actually, so don't let's have any of your fussing about, Billy.' He glanced at his watch. 'I'm shooting over old Fairhead's roots this afternoon with the C.O.' He lit a cigarette and scrutinized the Summary of Evidence. 'Nice simple case of desertion of post, thank God.' He looked over the table. 'Ink? Yes.' He filled his fountain pen. 'Any God's amount of partridge on old Fairhead's land. Hasn't been shot over this season.' He blew his nose noisily. 'This blanket stinks.' He gathered the papers into a little pile. 'Right. Let's have the Members.'

The Senior Member and the Junior Member stepped forward and the President took their names.

'Been on a court-martial before?' he asked the Junior Member.

'No, sir.'

'Well, don't worry, old boy; you'll soon pick it up. Just listen and we'll get through it in no time at all. Are there any officers under instruction?'

'No, sir.'

'You fellows have seen this?' He held up the Summary of Evidence.

'Yes, sir.'

'Splendid. Who's defending?'

Captain Gerard gave his name.

The President lowered his voice. 'Is he pleading guilty or not guilty, old man?'

'Guilty, sir.'

'Praise the Lord.' He glanced at his watch. 'He hasn't a leg to stand on, of course; never saw a more watertight case. But you never know with these fellows.'

His pen lisped on the smooth paper as he wrote and he

muttered amiably to himself. The trees sighed gustily down the drive and the rain tapped on the windows and the spider crawled two or three inches up the wall. This was his third court-martial in a month, the President said. He thought it was time somebody else had a go. 'That bloody Staff Captain.' Nobody spoke. The fire whispered in the grate and the wind blew the smoke down the chimney into the room.

'That's about it,' he announced at last. 'Take your places, please, gentlemen, and we'll get on with it.' He shouted for the Court Orderly. 'March in the Accused and escort and all witnesses, please.'

The Provost Sergeant saluted and withdrew. In the corridor he brought them to attention and gave them quick march and right wheel and heads up and into the room and right wheel again and then halt and left turn so that they faced the Court. At that time all the men in the room wore their caps except the Accused, who was bareheaded.

Then the President read out the articles summoning the Court. Did the Accused object to be tried by the Major as President or by any of the Members? No. The Court was sworn in. The voices droned. And I do further swear that. Disclose or discover the vote or opinion. Except whereunto required. Spoken in unison, it was difficult to follow.

'March out all except the Accused.'

When they had gone, the President said to the Accused, 'Sit down, Elwes. And listen carefully. You are charged under Section Six of the Army Act with leaving your post as a sentry while on active service before you were regularly relieved, in that you,' now he read aloud from the Charge Sheet, 'at approximately twenty-three fifty-nine hours on the twenty-seventh October nineteen forty-one did intentionally leave your post as sentry on the southern jetty of Imbleness Harbour without being regularly relieved, and did not return until approximately o-one hundred hours on the twenty-eighth October nineteen forty-one.' He looked at the soldier. 'Do you plead guilty or not guilty to this charge?'

The soldier's eyes swung over to Captain Gerard.

'He pleads guilty,' said Captain Gerard.

'Yes, sir,' said the Accused.

The President asked him, 'Do you understand what is meant by a plea of guilty? Do you understand that if you plead guilty the Court has no option but to find you guilty?'

'Yes, sir.'

'Does he?' the President asked the Defending Officer.

'Yes, sir, he does.'

'All right. The Court is closed.'

The Court Orderly marched the Accused from the room, and the Adjutant and Captain Gerard followed him out because they were not Members of the Court. It was not necessary to close the Court at that time.

'I'm dying for a smoke,' the President said. 'I didn't think it was necessary to read out the Summary of Evidence. It's perfectly watertight.' The members relaxed. They lit cigarettes and the President stared out of the window. 'Hope to God this rain lifts.' He looked at his watch.

The Junior Member thought of how he felt about the

Accused. Poor devil, he thought. They would be about the same age; the Accused was a little older maybe. Poor, lost, bewildered child. He was so damned pitiable. The Junior Member was fascinated and repelled by the immensity of his power over the Accused, and by the power he represented: Authority, the great Bogy, the ponderous unidentifiable They. What earthly chance had this frightened creature against such a monstrous host? The Junior Member had been prepared for a shifty-eyed bullet-headed killer, a barrack-room lawyer with the accents of Brooklyn or Chicago or the Mile End Road and an evil record. And this fair-headed child sat there in the chair and listened to the President and the tattered majesty of the oaths and looked with slow wide eyes from one to the other of the Court and understood nothing, not his own crime nor why he would be punished, not the confident spleen of the Adjutant nor the helplessness of Captain Gerard in the face of such evidence; not anything about it. He would go where they sent him and do as he was told. He would go to York, the Junior Member supposed, or to the Glasshouse in Aldershot, and there he would run all day, never walk, and scrub his equipment and then scrub it again till it was white and then again and again and then scrub floors and tables and be drilled and never be left alone for a minute from dawn until he was put to bed and earn good-conduct marks because he would not understand anything about it. Then he would return to his battalion and go on living exactly as he had lived before, hopelessly, pathetically lost in the gaunt black forest of un-understood motives. The Junior

Member brought himself up with a jolt. Damn it, the man had committed a crime whose results, in only slightly different circumstances, might have jeopardized the lives of tens of thousands of men, the success of a vast operation, perhaps the security of England itself, and he must be punished so that he would not do it again and so that others would not do it. That was all. There was nothing else to consider. He hoped the man felt no resentment or bitterness against him personally. He was about to administer justice. In that there could be no shame. It had no other aspects.

The President recalled the Accused and the two officers. They took their places in silence and the Court Orderly stood at ease by the door.

'Does the Accused wish to make a Statement in Mitigation?'

'Yes, sir,' Captain Gerard replied. 'If I may make it on his behalf.'

'You may. Is it made on oath? If the Statement is made on oath it will, of course, carry more weight with the Court than if it is not made on oath. But it is subject to cross-examination by the Prosecution. You may, if you wish, make the Statement without the oath; in that case the Prosecution may not examine.' He looked at his watch.

'On oath, sir.'

'Have you written it out?'

'Yes, sir.'

'Splendid. Good fellow. Saves any amount of time. Go ahead. Read it to the Court.'

Captain Gerard rose and cleared his throat.

'The plea of guilty, gentlemen,' he began, 'was made in the first place because there appeared to be little point in contesting evidence conclusive of physical guilt, of guilt, that is to say, in terms of time and circumstance. Of moral guilt, if any, I will have more to say later.'

The President eased himself forward in his chair.

'In the second place, the Accused pleaded guilty because, not unnaturally, he wished to avail himself of the clemency that such a plea lawfully merits. Now let us examine the charge for a moment. At the risk of the Court's displeasure I must say outright that there is no other word than trivial with which to describe the charge. Fifty minutes' absence, gentlemen. It is what one might reasonably call a routine charge. It has the quality of a charge that is made as a matter of course, rather than as a matter of prevention or cure.'

The Adjutant drew lines on the clean pink blotting-paper and pulled at his moustache.

'There is a saying in the Army of which I beg to remind the Court — I have heard it in civil life also: that all men are honest until they are found out. I have heard a Warrant Officer of twenty years' service describe his military career as having been one of twenty years of undetected crime. By that Warrant Officer the Accused would be described either as unlucky or as positively stupid, for the circumstances of the arrest were such that he might very easily have lied his way out of it. That he did not do so is something of a pointer to the extent of his moral guilt. He did not forbear to lie out of pure bravado; it is not in the man's character to avoid punishment, and he obviously had little idea of the possible consequence of his offence. I speak from first-hand knowledge of the Accused. I am his Company Commander and have been for a year. It is, indeed, my honest opinion that the charge could have been dealt with adequately without recourse to court-martial.'

He had it in mind to say: why, then, was the charge made? He had intended to suggest for the Court's consideration that the events of the night of the twenty-seventh of October, though quite beyond the control and responsibility of the Accused, seemed to call for blood. A head must roll. Somebody must be blamed. But he did not say it. It would do no good.

The voice rose and fell with the monotony of an oriental song and had the same soporific quality. Elwes strove to keep his eyes open. They had gone to all this trouble over him; it was only fair that he should listen. He watched the spider crawling up the wall behind the President's chair. Now it was almost level with the sash of the window through which he could see the tops of tall trees waving and the grey clouds.

'I submit for the Court's consideration that had the *Ur of the Chaldees* not sailed from Imbleness Harbour that night, the Accused would not be faced with this charge now. And yet the departure of the ship and the Accused's absence from his post were not in any way connected. The one was not the result of the other.'

Elwes was startled when the Adjutant said, 'I object to that.'

'On what grounds?' the President asked him.

'It's irrelevant, to begin with.'

'The defence is to be allowed every possible latitude.'

Elwes felt embarrassed that he had caused them all this trouble and he wished they would finish it off quickly. He did not understand why they had to go through all this. Had he not already pleaded guilty? He wanted them to sentence him and then leave him alone, for their own sakes, for the sake of the President, who had spoken to him civilly and was in such a hurry, for the Captain, who was so bored, for the young Lieutenant, especially for him, he was so obviously feeling sorry for the Accused. In this officer's eyes there was too much pity. Elwes did not expect pity nor did he want it. It was extremely embarrassing to be pitied. He resented it a little. In fact, the boot was on the other foot; it was Elwes who felt sorry for the officer. The Lieutenant did not understand the way Elwes felt about him, that was plain, and Elwes would have liked to tell him, I am all right, thank you, I am in excellent health, with some asperity. What you are doing is right and just; don't feel badly about it. I neither expect nor want your sympathy. I'm fine. Right now nothing worries me. I am all right, you see, inside. My heart is undisturbed. For I am armoured now. I know more than you know. You are quite powerless to touch me. Stop pitying me now, for it is I who pity you. Your position is an awfully difficult one, but don't make it worse for yourself.

The voice buzzed and droned. 'Because the Accused loves music. He loves music as other men love beer; as the

President, if I may point the moral, loves shooting birds.'

He wished the Captain would stop now. He was getting himself into trouble. The whole thing was trouble for everybody, for Captain Gerard and Foster and Winslow and the other men and everybody. For Christ's sake, Corporal Foster had asked him, why didn't you tell me you wanted to go? Any of the lads would have mucked in for you for an hour, you know that; damn it, I'd have done it myself. Why didn't you tell me? Why? Why?

'Finally, I would ask the Court to give particular consideration to the effect of anything more than the very minimum sentence on this man. Consider the effect of a routine sentence for a routine crime in a routine punishment camp among routine criminals. What would be the effect of such an environment on a sensitive boy, a boy whose character is not, thank God, routine? It is an unhappy fact that military detention camps are filled in the majority by men who have been there before. To condemn this boy to live for a long period among, to absorb the vile philosophy of, to become at one with, men of that ilk, many of them already hardened civil criminals, is a crime in itself, a shocking repudiation of the understanding and tolerance that is the very spirit of this new army of ours. Let us not make another of these men. We have enough to answer for, God knows. The life we live is of our own building, and two wars in half a lifetime is much for which to ask forgiveness. Elwes and his generation have little to thank us for. Let us not make their job worse, for there are not too many of them and we have arranged to kill a large number. We, gentlemen, you and I, are finished. You might say, we have had it. We're a curious sort of growth, neither malignant nor wholly harmless. We belong nowhere, not even in history, for in time our two wars will come together as one and we who have lived between will be forgotten. For God's sake let us not drag down this boy with us, nor any like him. He is the hope of the world. He may succeed where we have failed. Out of the pit a little light may come, if we allow. It has no name, this quality which I believe to be in Elwes; the quality of common humanity perhaps. But perhaps Elwes will find it for us, and pin it down, and name it, and use it. It's not in him alone. It is in all men and all things, in the rich and poor alike, in the wise and the ignorant and the foolish, in the leaders and in the led, in good men and bad men, in the souls of men in duress, and always in the young soldier. Let us cherish it.'

He hesitated and then sat down, knowing it was hopeless.

The President looked at the Prosecuting Officer and the Adjutant rose to his feet. He coughed, and then he said,

'Gentlemen, the enemy is at Calais.'

With startling sickening suddenness the spider lost its hold on the wall and fell, as if the Adjutant's word had held some special surprise for it, and Elwes thought back to the officer's statement, for though he had heard it clearly enough it had had no meaning. What had he said? Gentlemen, the enemy is at Calais. That was it. Well, it was certainly correct. The enemy is at Calais. Certainly. Whoever said the enemy was not? The officer had said it as though such a thing were unheard-of. The enemy has always been at Calais. One might as well say that London is on the Thames. No, that was not the same; that did not quite follow. Fair do's. No, what I mean is, everybody knows the enemy is at Calais. It is almost a tenet of war, and to be expected. One would be surprised indeed if the enemy were not at Calais. After all, you could not fight for a chance to fight for something if the enemy were not available. But what am I fighting for a chance to fight for? The familiar question swam in his mind like a goldfish towing a pale train of glory and gaped at him and swam away again but never out of his mind and then returned with the roseate glory following and hovered over his eyes. It had been there a long time now. Captain Gerard ought to have been more explicit. He closed his eyes.

'Pay attention,' the President said sharply.

He opened his eyes and felt the colour rising to his cheeks.

He was surprised at the bitterness in the Adjutant's voice and at his own indifference. It seemed that his offence had been in the nature of a personal affront to the Adjutant, whereas he himself believed it to have been an offence against himself only, a betrayal of his spirit for which he would be punished dispassionately by others whose motives were pure, impersonal, automatic. He was no more disturbed by the Adjutant's passion than by the pity in the eyes of the Junior Member. It was astonishing, this sudden inviolability. He knew whence it came; he was busy elsewhere, that was it. He had too much to think about. He had been given a question and the answer was within his grasp, but until he understood it fully — and so far its full significance escaped him—he was insensitive to all else. No matter how long it might take to find the answer, there was no escape from the necessity.

When the Court had been cleared, the President stretched and looked at his watch and said, 'Just nice time.' He lit a cigarette.

'The Defending Officer was good, I thought,' the Senior Member remarked.

'I'm afraid he's going to find himself on the carpet.'

The Junior Member said nothing.

'Well now,' the President began briskly, 'the question of sentence. Let me sum up one or two things for you.' He stared out of the window. 'By God, it's stopped raining.' He rose and went to the window and looked up at the sky. 'It's clearing up.'

The Members waited.

'Sentence. Sentence.' Now he stood warming his legs at the fire. 'The sentence, gentlemen. Well, there are several things to consider. Let us take the pro's first. As the Defending Officer said, the extent of the moral guilt isn't very great. The chap came back of his own accord and the thing was probably done on the spur of the moment anyway.

Impulse. We all have impulses occasionally. He seems a
decent kid, very young, very young indeed. And it's a first
offence. He probably wouldn't do it again in a thousand
years. He only cleared off for fifty minutes, when all's said
and done.'

The Senior Member interrupted, 'He could have lied
his way out of it, no doubt about it.'

'Quite. Quite so. Can't understand why he didn't myself.
However. He's probably a bit dumb. But why did he clear
off? I must say, I was a bit shaken when I saw the Summary
of Evidence. Fiddling while Rome burns and so forth. He
knows things are pretty tough with the Boche twenty-odd
miles away from England. It's a bit thick, scraping a fiddle
just now. It's not a thing I'd run around shouting about,
myself, in any case. Probably a shade neurotic, in which
case a dose of detention might do him a lot of good. Then
there's another thing we should consider: what does the
man's C.O. want? How does he want him dealt with?
Obviously pretty stiffly, or he wouldn't have asked for a
court-martial. You want to bear that in mind. Then again,
there's a bit of paper from division circulating around,
don't know if you've seen it, saying there's a prevalence
of this sort of crime just now, desertion of post and absence
and so on, and courts-martial aren't lashing out enough.
Sentences are too light and we've got to come down pretty
hard on these fellows. That's another thing to keep in mind.
And remember we don't decide the sentence finally. It has
to be approved by the Brigadier and he can always decrease
any punishment we award. Commute it. He can't increase

it. So it's better, if anything, to err on the heavy side, then
the Brigadier can cut it down if he thinks fit. Think it over.
I'll give you a couple of minutes.'

And in the yard, Elwes asked the Court Orderly,

'When will I know?'

'Got to be promulgated. Maybe a week.'

Elwes nodded.

The leaves fluttered from the trees in the drive and
the treetops moved in the wind and the rain came down
steadily.